Morgan stared up at him, then let a breath go in a heavy sigh

"I'm sorry. I talk too much. I get too passionate about things. I get carried away. I'm sorry."

Ethan met her blue eyes and wondered what it would be like if her passion was directed at him and not this land business. What if it was just between the two of them? "Let's go," he said, and went to the door.

He didn't know the answer to that question now, but he was definitely going to find out.

Dear Reader,

Going home is something we all dream about, no matter how far away that home is. But to find a home when you didn't even realize it was there waiting for you is very special. In *Home to the Doctor,* Ethan Grace, a direct ancestor of a famous pirate from the eighteenth century, lives all over the country, but when he goes back to an estate he has on Shelter Island in Puget Sound, Washington, it's to rest and recuperate after an accident. He doesn't even think he's going home. He can't wait to heal and leave… until he meets Dr. Morgan Kelly.

Morgan went back to the island to help her father, the local physician, and has no intention of staying there—at least, not until her dad retires. But when Ethan and Morgan meet, first as adversaries, then as lovers, home takes on a whole new meaning. The most unexpected twists of fate make our lives what they become, and Morgan and Ethan find a life together that neither ever dreamed was possible. And a real home in each other.

I hope you enjoy Morgan and Ethan's story, and that you will watch for the last installment of the SHELTER ISLAND STORIES—*Home for a Hero.*

Mary Anne Wilson

Home to the Doctor
MARY ANNE WILSON

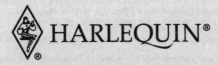

TORONTO • NEW YORK • LONDON
AMSTERDAM • PARIS • SYDNEY • HAMBURG
STOCKHOLM • ATHENS • TOKYO • MILAN • MADRID
PRAGUE • WARSAW • BUDAPEST • AUCKLAND

ISBN-13: 978-0-373-75175-4
ISBN-10:   0-373-75175-3

HOME TO THE DOCTOR

This edition published by arrangement with Harlequin Books S.A.

® and TM are trademarks of the publisher. Trademarks indicated with ® are registered in the United States Patent and Trademark Office, the Canadian Trade Marks Office and in other countries.

www.eHarlequin.com

Printed in U.S.A.

ABOUT THE AUTHOR

Mary Anne Wilson is a Canadian transplanted to Southern California, where she lives with her husband, three children and an assortment of animals. She knew she wanted to write romances when she found herself "rewriting" the great stories in literature, such as *A Tale of Two Cities*, to give them "happy endings." Over her long career she's published more than thirty romances, had her books on bestseller lists, been nominated for Reviewer's Choice Awards and received a career nomination in romantic suspense. She's looking forward to her next thirty books.

Books by Mary Anne Wilson

HARLEQUIN AMERICAN ROMANCE

Don't miss any of our special offers. Write to us at the following address for information on our newest releases.

Harlequin Reader Service
U.S.: 3010 Walden Ave., P.O. Box 1325, Buffalo, NY 14269
Canadian: P.O. Box 609, Fort Erie, Ont. L2A 5X3

For everyone who dreams of going home...
and realizes that dream

Chapter One

As a doctor, Morgan Kelly was more than familiar with the male body and couldn't really remember the last time she'd looked at a man as anything other than a patient or a curiosity. But as she walked alone on the hard sand of the beach on Shelter Island in Puget Sound and lifted her face into the cold December air, she stopped in her tracks. A naked man was standing thirty feet above her.

At least she thought he was naked. He was on the decking of a guest house on an exclusive estate, and the wooden railing hit him just below his waist. From the distance and in the rapidly failing light of the day, she couldn't make out his features enough to know if she recognized him or not, but she definitely could tell his stomach, chest, broad shoulders and strong arms were bare. The temperature had to be in the fifties, but he didn't seem to notice at all. It was as if the bitter wind blowing over the choppy, dark waters of the sound didn't exist.

He stared out across the sound to the mainland of Washington State before he glanced north, then south. For a fleeting moment she was certain as his gaze came toward her, that he saw her, a lone figure, all five feet three inches of her in her faded college sweatshirt, jeans and heavy boots, her flame-red hair pulled into a ponytail. But he didn't react to her

presence if he did. Instead he looked back across the waters
playing around her boots.

He cupped his hands at his eyes, and she thought she saw
a dark mark on his left shoulder, then thunder sounded and
she looked away to the heavy gray of the sky above. A few
centuries ago, the noise would have been the roar of a cannon
that famed pirate Bartholomew Grace would have fired at his
enemies who dared to disturb the peace of his Shelter Island
refuge. The original owner of most of the island, old Bartholomew had come here every fall, staying until spring, either to
celebrate his victories if he'd had a successful campaign in
the south, or to recoup from his losses if fate had turned
against him on the high seas.

But this wasn't where Bartholomew would have been
scanning the horizon; he would have been in one of the turrets
of the main house. She'd only seen the house from her father's
boat when they'd been on the sound, and from a distance it
looked for all the world like a castle. Its multiple turrets
towering in the air, the home was built out of rock, stone and
dark wood. This stranger had to be staying in the guest house
she'd been told was on the property.

Instead of pirates occupying the house and land now,
Bartholomew's descendants, Anthony and Celia Grace, did,
along with their only child, Ethan. They'd lived on the island
for as long as Morgan could remember. But since she'd left
ten years ago, things had changed. She'd heard that Ethan's
parents had taken off to Europe about five years ago and had
been back only once or twice. Their son seemed to have in-
herited the estate, but he returned sporadically, too. The
thought that he was the man at the railing came and went;
Ethan Grace wouldn't be staying in the guest house.

Most of the year he lived on the mainland and, depending
on who you asked among the locals, that meant Seattle, or Los

Angeles, or San Francisco or New York. Maybe he had residences in all those places; he certainly had the finances to live wherever he wanted. He'd taken over as head of the corporation his grandfather, then his father, had run, and according to her own father, that company "ate up and spit out everything in its path." He'd made a comment about the pirate's occupation being revisited on his descendants, and that Ethan used money and the law as his weapons while Bartholomew had used gunpowder and swords.

She'd walked these beaches all of her life before she'd left for college, but this was her first exploration since her father had asked her to come home. She'd arrived a week ago and loved to be finally doing what she called "beach wandering." She paid no attention to the Private Beach signs she'd passed before seeing the man. Maybe he was an early arrival for the big wedding reception Ethan was giving for his friend Joe Lawrence, another islander who had come back about six months ago.

There was a lot of gossip from her father's patients and the people she knew in town about Joe's wedding to Alegra Reynolds, the founder of the Alegra's Closet boutiques. They'd marry privately, then have their reception at the Grace estate. Some of the locals had been sent invitations, but Morgan wasn't among them. No reason she would be; neither Joe Lawrence, nor Ethan Grace had been in her circle of friends in the old days.

There was a flash of lightning in the east, then more thunder rolled across the heavens, shaking the air around her. She looked up and down the beach, then decided to head back. She stepped toward the water and couldn't resist looking up again. The man was still there despite the growing cold that was cutting through her sweatshirt and his decided lack of clothes. She exhaled, unaware until then that she'd been holding her breath, then she turned to the water. She was reluctant to go back to the office and check the phone service. She had her cell phone in her pocket, but even so, she felt the weight of the responsibility of being the only doctor on the island at the moment. Her father was on his first vacation in years—one unplanned when a good friend had invited him to visit—and she'd agreed to come back and take over his practice until he returned. Simple, right? But it was anything but simple.

She watched the lights on the mainland flashing to life through the gathering mists of dusk, and could smell the hint of rain in the air. She liked rain. She liked the moods of the island. Maybe the weather wouldn't be good for the up-coming reception, but it would be good for her. Even the rich Graces couldn't control the weather, especially on Shelter Island.

She finally turned to walk back up the beach, deciding to go directly to the office. But she had only taken a few steps when she was startled by a loud crash that had nothing to do with the impending storm, but it did come from above her. A deep male voice yelled at the same time, and although she couldn't quite make out the words, she had no doubt from the tone, that that might be for the best. She turned and moved closer to the water so she could get a better angle to look up at the decking.

She stared hard, trying to make out any movement, but all she could see were lights that were on in the house now. She turned to leave, but as soon as she took a step, another crash came from the house. It sounded like glass breaking this time, along with something heavy hitting an unforgiving surface. But this time, there was no yelling, just the low sound of foghorns over the water and the cry of a night bird in the air.

She could have kept walking, and would have if she hadn't finally heard someone scream in anger or pain or both. That drove her to change all her plans. She looked around and spotted a series of broad steps that led to the top of the bluffs defined by lights so dim they were little more than a blur. Jogging over to the well-fashioned stairs in the rock wall, she grabbed the cold damp metal railing that ran up one side.

She climbed as quickly as she could, not at all sure what she'd find at the top, but images of a naked man lying prone on the deck, bloodied and in pain, flashed in her mind. She'd look to make sure everything was all right, then she'd leave. Being a doctor, she'd learned that you offered help first and worried later about the details. The worst that could happen was that some burly bodyguard would "usher" her off of the estate.

She stepped out at the top onto an expanse of deep emerald grass, dotted by thick ferns hugging the ground and wind-twisted pines along with madrone trees. The main house, which was two hundred feet back from the bluffs and beyond a stone terrace, loomed high into the dusky sky, looking like some monstrous castle as it had from the waters. Light through the multipaned windows was concentrated in the central area, creating a series of glowing strips. Heavy drapes that covered French doors were partially pushed aside. In the low light, the structure looked foreboding and unsettling. It didn't look like home sweet home at all.

To her left and fifty yards or so along the bluff's edge, Morgan saw the guest house that overlooked the beach. At least that bit of structure wasn't hidden behind trees, shrubs and ferns. She spotted a portion of the deck to the left and a stone walkway that cut a meandering path through the ankle-deep grass and separated to go to the back toward the deck and to the front of the house. She hurried along the path, avoiding the low limbs of old trees, and hesitated at the fork, finally choosing the direction of the deck.

She took two wooden steps up onto the deck that seemed

to shoot right out into the air, with no visible signs of the heavy supports she knew were below it. Interior light spilled out of a pair of open French doors, and showed at least one reason for the crashes she'd heard. What had been a huge potted plant moments ago was now a heap of broken pottery, scattered soil and a huge, thick-leafed tree of some sort lying askew. She crossed to the mess, and carefully picked her way around the pottery shards, to get to the open doors.

She grabbed the door frame and almost stepped in, but stopped when she saw the second cause of the noise—a heavy leather chair had been upended along with a small side table. A lamp that had probably been some sort of Tiffany antique was shattered beyond hope of restoration. Broken pieces of bright glass scattered in a wide arc on the polished wooden floor.

She looked into an expansive room with polished wood floors, furniture in supple leather and dark woods arranged in front of a stone fireplace to the left, and more antique furniture set to get the most of the view of the sound. Paintings on the rough plaster walls were either great prints or the originals. She'd bet on them being originals.

She carefully stepped past the chair and to one side of the broken glass, then called out "Hello?" before noticing traces of dirt smeared on the floor as if something had been dragged through both messes. Whatever had done the damage had been heading to steps that led up to a set of partially ajar doors. She touched the closest door and it swung back silently.

"Hello?" she called again, and was slightly surprised when she heard a muffled response from a deep male voice.

"In here."

She took the steps in one stride and found herself in a huge bedroom space. She barely noticed the heavy antique furnishings or the fact that the area was a true suite, with open rooms off both sides and a circular staircase near the middle of the room that led upward to another level.

All she really saw was the man from the porch sitting on the dark, polished wooden floor at the foot of a bed that would have been appropriate for Bartholomew Grace's boudoir. It was huge, made of dark, intricately carved wood, with heavy drapes at all four posts and a mattress that sat a good three feet off the floor. She focused on the man slumped against the side of the bed, the partial cast on his left leg and his skin, which was sleek with sweat despite the definite chill in the room. His eyes were closed tightly, and his face looked oddly flushed and pale at the same time. She knew that look— he was in real pain.

She hurried over to him, crouched and automatically took in his rapid breathing, his clenched jaw and erratic pulse. At some point she realized he wasn't actually naked but wore a pair of khaki shorts. He also wasn't just anyone. He was Ethan Grace.

"What's going on?" she asked, knowing that he'd been aware of her presence when he didn't flinch at the sound of her voice or even open his eyes.

"Get my medication. It's in the bathroom." He rasped out the order.

She didn't take any offense at the rude demand; pain changed everything. "Of course," she said, "but first, let me get you up off the floor."

She scooted closer and reached out to him. She might only weigh a hundred and ten pounds at the most, but she was used to lifting patients twice her size. She'd guessed he was around a hundred and ninety pounds, maybe six feet two or three inches tall. She hadn't seen Ethan Grace for years, but she had no doubt she was helping the man who owned all of this. And that man didn't have a smudge on his upper arm but a tattoo, which surprised her as she looked at the four-inch-long dagger with a snake twined around it. Beneath it was the script "Do It."

When she touched the tattoo, he jerked at the contact and his eyes flew open. Deep brown eyes, almost black. He looked confused, then said in a tight voice, "What in the hell?"

His dark brown hair was clinging damply to his flushed face that seemed all sharp angles and his jaw was shadowed by the beginnings of a new beard. He looked strong and capable, but she knew that even the strongest man couldn't help himself when pain took over. She tried to be reassuring as she said, "Okay, we can do this," while carefully straddling his legs and attempting to push her hands under his arms.

His skin was hot to the touch. No wonder he had the doors wide-open. She needed to get him in bed, then find the medication he mentioned.

"Mr. Grace, I'm going to get you up and onto the bed." She braced herself, took a deep breath and pushed as hard as she could with her legs. But nothing worked.

Even with his dead weight, she could have lifted him, but he barely moved up before his momentum pulled her back and toward him. She felt her feet slip on the hardwood floor, and in that moment, she knew that she was going to fall onto him.

Deliberately she let go of him and threw herself to her right as far as she could so her legs wouldn't make more contact with him than they already were. She tumbled to the floor, hitting her shoulder hard, but as she landed she knew that she'd managed to keep off of his legs.

She twisted to look at him, saw those black eyes on her. She was sitting on the floor by Ethan Grace, in a guest house and trying to figure out how to get him into bed.

ETHAN WASN'T SURE what the hell was going on. It seemed that there was a woman with him, a stranger, almost sitting on top of him and calling him Mr. Grace. This small redhead wasn't Natalie. No, Natalie was in L.A. on a case. Or maybe she was in Europe. He couldn't remember. And Natalie never would have worn a sweatshirt and jeans and certainly wouldn't have called him Mr. Grace. His mind was so damn foggy from the pain. Then the woman was pulling him, making pain shoot up his leg, making him almost nauseated.

She was suddenly gone as if she'd fallen off the edge of his world, and he was back on the floor surrounded by the throb of bone-deep pain. No, she was still there, close by, talking in a breathless voice. "I'd say that didn't go well."

What hadn't gone well? He frowned, then she was in front of him again, crouching over him, her hand on his forehead, her fingers pressed to the hollow of his throat. "You have to get into the bed," she was saying. "And you have to help me."

Forget the bed. "Who are you?" he muttered, each word causing him more agony.

"I'm a doctor," she said.

He closed his eyes tightly, trying to control his pain, as well as blot out the weirdness of what was going on in front of him. He had to be hallucinating. A doctor? With flaming-red hair? A doctor in some sort of sweat outfit? A doctor who'd been trying to sit in his lap? Ethan forced himself to open his eyes again and focus. "How?" he said, intending to ask her how she got here.

But she said, "Tons of medical school and hard work." He couldn't have smiled to save his life. "Now, you have to help me get you into bed."

Sure, and he could fly if he jumped off the deck, he thought. He couldn't move, let alone get onto the bed. If he even tried to sit straight, the pain increased. "No, I…"

She was standing over him again, and he tried to focus on her, but his vision was blurry and the world had a halo of gray around everything. "I'll help you, but you have to help me," she said, and her hands were on him again, at his chest, slipping under his arms. "Push as much as you can and try to lean toward me." He realized her cheek was against his, and her mouth was by his ear. "All right?"

Before he could agree or disagree, she was actually lifting him up. He was amazed that this tiny person who was supposed to be a doctor managed to get him into the cool linens of the bed. Pain burned through him when he hit the sheets, but the next instant, it eased and he found he could actually breathe. Was he doing it all himself, or imagining the doctor was doing it for him? Had he hallucinated the whole thing? Catching his cast on the plant, the fall, then trying to get inside, another fall, then this woman sitting in his lap?

"It's okay," she whispered from somewhere above him, but he couldn't even muster the strength to open his eyes for a moment. "It's okay."

His good leg was being raised onto the bed, then his broken leg was miraculously positioned on the bed, too. The pain was circling him now but no longer cutting in to him. He kept breathing as evenly as he possibly could. He didn't move until he felt a hand on his forehead, a soft touch that was gone quickly. "Where's your medication?" she asked him.

Without opening his eyes, he muttered, "Bathroom."

He could sense the emptiness where she'd been or where he'd imagined she'd been when she left. Just when he thought he'd lost it, that there was no one here but him, the red-haired doctor was back. She slipped a hand under his neck and shoulders, helped him up a bit, then said, "Open your mouth, Mr. Grace."

"Ethan," he mumbled right before he did as he was told and felt two pills fall onto his tongue. Then the coolness of a glass rim was against his lips and cold water slipped down his throat. She lowered him gently onto the bed, and in a moment, she was speaking to him. "Put your arms around my neck. Hold on and let me maneuver you up and back so I can adjust your leg."

When he opened his eyes, the blurred image was breathtaking. Brilliant hair, blue eyes, hands on his shoulder, her breath brushing his clammy skin. Put his arms around her? He didn't hesitate. He slipped his hands onto her shoulders and behind her neck. He felt her hair brush his bare skin as she shifted, practically hugging him to her with one arm.

He heard her whispering over and over again, "Just a bit farther, just a bit, just a bit." He felt his hands start to slip, and he tried to get a new grip on her, but it didn't work. His hands balled up her sweatshirt, and she was falling toward him, the way he'd thought she had on the floor. But this time she didn't just disappear to one side; she landed on his stomach and chest. The scent of flowers seemed to be everywhere, and the weight of her on him wasn't painful at all.

If it all was a hallucination, it was one hell of a hallucination, he thought. She slipped away from him again. He didn't have the strength to reach out for her this time. It was all he could do to open his eyes and look up to find her bending over him. "The pills should work quickly," she said in a soft voice that seemed to drift around him.

"Where…" He licked his lips. "Where did you come from?"

"The beach. I was walking." The words echoed in the room as if bouncing back off the fog that was creeping into his line of vision. "I heard the crashes and thought you needed help."

Help? That fog was creeping closer and closer, the way it had off the sound so many times. But he was in the guest house. And there was a woman with him. Not Natalie. Standing over him, with the gentlest voice and touch.

He closed his eyes again when it became too hard to keep them open. "I fell," was all he could get past his lips.

"I heard," she murmured as her hand touched his forehead,

smoothed back his hair. "Can I call someone?" Her voice seemed farther away and muffled now.

"No," he said. "No." He settled deeper into the grayness. "Just need sleep."

There was no voice now, and he had that same feeling that he'd had before, that empty sensation when he knew he really was alone. Whatever had happened, it was done. Whatever he'd dreamed or hallucinated was gone. The woman, whoever she was or hadn't been, wasn't there, and he fell into a sleep that came in a rush of relief from the pain.

Chapter Two

Ethan woke slowly and did what he had done every morning since his accident—he kept his eyes closed, measuring the pain to test the levels of discomfort he'd be facing that day. This time he felt a dull throb that ran the length of his injured leg, from his foot to his hip, but it was bearable. Then he remembered the fall and the aftermath. He opened his eyes to glance around the bedroom in the guest house, where he'd moved to from his suite in the main building basically to avoid the confusion of the preparations for Joey's wedding reception.

He'd been tired of the chaos everywhere, and had yet to understand why so many people were needed to pull off a party that would last for two or three hours tops, two weeks from now. He'd do anything for Joe, but enduring the insanity all around him while he was healing and trying to work hadn't been possible. So he'd taken over the guest house on the bluffs.

And regretted ever driving himself in the Jaguar. He should have waited for James Evans, his assistant and friend for the past ten years, to come back from a late-day appointment. Then Ethan wouldn't have been outside his corporate building when a car swerved to miss a pedestrian and broadsided him as he'd pulled out of the underground parking and onto the street. The speed hadn't been great and the Jaguar had been heavy enough to take the impact, but if he hadn't gotten out right away to check the damage, he wouldn't have gotten pinned between the two cars. The other driver had jumped out of his car and forgotten to put it in Park. Before Ethan knew what was happening, he had a broken leg.

"You're pretty lucky to get out of it with a simple fracture," his doctor had told him. When Ethan had challenged Doctor Maury Perry's definition of *lucky,* the man who had been his physician for over ten years had shrugged philosophically. "You're alive, it's a clean break and you won't be off your feet too long. You're damn lucky, Ethan."

Ethan had never bought in to the idea of luck. If luck had been involved, there wouldn't have been an accident. He exhaled, assured that the pain wasn't going to get worse any time soon, and twisted his head to see his medication and a half-full glass of water by the bed.

An image flashed in his mind of someone lifting him, giving him pills and cold water. Then he remembered. Tripping. Falling. The pain exploding. Almost crawling into the house. The table and chair crashing to the floor, the lamp breaking. The red-haired woman coming to him out of nowhere, helping him, sitting on top of him. Or maybe not. Maybe he'd dreamed it, or maybe the pills had made him hallucinate. But he wasn't imagining being in bed with his broken leg raised on a couple of pillows. And his prescription and water were right by him.

Had the doctor done that?

He raised himself carefully on one elbow to look around. He was sure the chair had fallen over, but now it was sitting by the door, right along with the side table. The only clue he had that the accident had happened at all was the missing Tiffany lamp, which he remembered shattering.

He glanced at the French doors. They were shut. He checked the clock by the bed. Six-thirty. The light coming in the back windows was dull and gray, and he could see the rain streaking the glass. He reached for the service button Jim had rigged on the side of the headboard, the button he'd been trying to get to last night when he'd passed out on the floor by the bed. He pressed it, then fell back into the bed and closed his eyes. His leg was throbbing steadily, and he felt confused. He hated both sensations, but more than that, he hated not knowing exactly what had happened the previous evening.

In less than five minutes, James came striding into the guest house. The man was large, matching Ethan's six-foot-two-inch frame, but outweighing him by a good thirty pounds. James wasn't given to much physical activity unless it was a rousing game of chess, but he always wore running shoes. He was dressed as usual in a casual polo shirt, dark slacks and white sneakers. He brushed his prematurely gray hair straight back from his square face, and his pale blue eyes flicked over his boss as he came closer to the high bed.

"Good morning, sunshine," he said with a gusto that grated on Ethan's frayed nerves. "How are we doing today? Or should I say, who are we doing today?" He didn't wait for a response. "Ginnero is waiting on your decision on the money, and if you could, let Bruce know what you are going to do about approaching the Wakefield Group. He's in Mexico now." James was invaluable, never forgetting anything, yet dealing with the business in an almost offhanded manner. "You really need to put these people out of their misery, boss."

"Later," Ethan murmured and gingerly pushed himself up, feeling a twinge in his leg when it slipped off the pillows that had been supporting it. He grimaced but kept moving to sit up against the headboard.

James proceeded to stuff pillows behind Ethan's back, then adjusted the ones that had been under his injured leg. "Good idea to elevate your leg," he said as he stood back. "Isn't that what the doctor said to do, along with resting as much as you can?"

Yes, Dr. Perry had said that very thing, but it hadn't been Ethan's idea to do it. "Were you down here last night?"

"Last night?" James asked. "No. I told you I was going to the city to see…a friend. Julie, the dental assistant." Ethan nodded and James went on. "I took the first ferry back this morning. Just walked into my room when the bell went off and I came on down here. Why?"

"I took a fall."

James frowned at Ethan. "What were you doing to fall?"

"I was trying to walk. I went onto the deck, wondering why the hell I agreed to come here to recuperate at all. When I turned to come back in, the damn cast hit a potted plant. I ended up on my behind."

James was all business now. "I'll call Dr. Perry, and then get Scooter to bring the helicopter over right away."

"No," Ethan said quickly. "Forget that. I'm okay." He was so sick of being sick and even sicker of doctors. At least, most doctors. "There was a doctor here already."

James looked confused now. "The local doctor?"

"No," he said, remembering Dr. Andrew Kelly from his childhood, a pleasant man with thinning sandy hair and a quiet manner. "No, it wasn't Dr. Kelly. It was a woman."

"She checked you out?"

"I think so," Ethan said, but couldn't remember her doing more than touching his forehead and being on top of him in the bed. "She got me settled," he said, "and I guess she got my medication." He glanced past James. "She must have picked up the mess I made over there, too."

"I thought you said you fell on the deck."

"I did, then I came in here, grabbed that chair by the door for balance, but I sent it over on its back with the side table and lamp."

"What lamp?" James asked, looking in the direction Ethan indicated.

"The one I broke when it fell."

"Hurricane Ethan," James muttered as he crossed to the French doors and opened them. "Well, you made a mess out here," he said, then closed the door and walked over to the phone by the spiral staircase. After dialing four digits and asking someone to come clean up the guest house, he came back to Ethan. "How did you get the doctor to visit?"

"I didn't. I think she was on the beach and came up to…" He wasn't sure why she'd come up or even if she actually had been there. The falls had been real, but maybe they'd knocked him senseless. Maybe he'd just imagined her being with him and her touch on his skin. Maybe the pills had conjured her up. He usually hated medication. "She was here," he said as much to assure himself as to answer James's question.

"Are you sure you don't want to check in with your own doctor?" James asked, either not noticing his uncertainty or not wanting to ignore it.

"No, I'm okay." He was. Although his leg was no better or no worse, his head was finally clear. He wouldn't take any medication again unless he absolutely had to. Besides, he had work to take care of, and one more thing he wanted to do. "Find out who the doctor is for me, will you?"

"Sure," James said, before changing the subject. "Want me to check your faxes and e-mails?"

"I'll do it," Ethan muttered. "I hate being out of the loop like this."

"Out of the loop? How? You've got every modern convenience in this place from the fax, to the high-speed Internet

connection and *four* computers, which are never turned off."
He shook his head. "Your receptionist is keeping your office
in the city going, and keeping you going out here. And isn't
Natalie going to show up sooner or later?" His grin turned a
bit mischievous. "At least as soon as you're up for her visit."

Ethan had had enough. "Natalie's going to come for the
wedding reception, then stick around. And my receptionist is
earning her pay. And my assortment of methods to keep in
contact just don't cut it. I never should have agreed to come
here in the first place."

"Well, you did. So suck it up, heal and get out of here,"
James said with a flippancy that no other employee would get
away with. "And quit falling over your cast. Now, are you
getting up, and do you need help dressing?"

"I'm getting up and I'm going to do just fine putting on
fresh shorts myself."

James glanced at Ethan's sole clothing, the beige shorts he'd
had on the day before. "Well, you might have had a doctor in
here, but she didn't get you in your jammies, did she?"

"Oh, knock it off," Ethan said and let his friend pull him
up and out of the bed. He stood there, carefully getting his
balance, then waved off James's support as he grabbed the
single crutch he hated using and made his way across the
room to the bathroom. "I'll be damn glad to have a real
shower when this thing comes off," he said.

"You're telling me," James said with an exaggerated sniff.
"I have to be around you."

Ethan laughed harshly at that attempt at a joke. When he
got into the bathroom, James retrieved the protective plastic
sleeve and bootie that fit over the cast so Ethan could at least
get in the shower, but keep the bottom part of his right leg dry.
James fitted it for him, then turned on the shower. "Take your
time," he said, closing the door behind him as he left.

"James?" Ethan said quickly.

The man peeked back in at him. "What now?"

"Don't forget to find out who the lady doctor was."

"Sure," he said, leaving.

Ethan got his shorts off, then limped into the shower stall and, keeping his right leg out of the direct stream of water, let the spray wash over his face. Closing his eyes, an oddly clear image of the lady doctor came to him. The red hair, the blue eyes. Then it blurred and was gone.

By the time Ethan was out of the shower, dried and had stripped off the plastic protection for his cast, James was knocking on the door. "What?" Ethan called out.

"Got some information on the doctor," he called through the closed door.

Ethan slipped on clean shorts and opened the door. "So, what do you have?" he asked, hobbling back into the room.

"A lady showed up at the main house last night, told Mrs. Forbes you'd taken a fall and that you were in bed. She said she was a doctor and that she'd given you pain pills and that it appeared you were going to be okay, but you might need to see your own physician in the morning."

Ethan felt great relief that the doctor had indeed been here, that she'd been real. The news settled something in him, and it also made him more curious about her. "She's a guest?"

"Not that the maid knew of. The doctor just told them to check on you. She mentioned the mess in the living room and on the deck, and that she thought you'd sleep through the night."

"What's her name?"

"Well, Estelle didn't know at first, but then a local woman, Sylvia something or other, who's here helping with the reception seemed to know her. She called her Morgan, and Estelle said they talked as if they were old friends."

This was taking too long. "Who is she?" he asked.

"I'm getting to that," James said patiently.

"Then do it." Ethan headed for a room to the right that was set up as an office for him. He sank down in the swivel leather chair, propped his cast on a low footstool James had found for him and didn't touch any of the computers or reach for the phone. James hung out by the door. Ethan looked right at him. "You know, I hate this about you. You hold on to information as if it's gold."

James just grinned. "I like knowing something you don't," he murmured.

Ethan picked up the crutch he'd laid against the desk and mimed holding it like a spear and aiming it at James. "Come on. I'm in no mood for games."

"Okay, okay," James said as he held out his palms toward Ethan in surrender, and the crutch went back to leaning against the desk. "Her name's Morgan Kelly." He paused, waited and when Ethan didn't show any sign of recognition, James continued. "She's the daughter of the local doctor."

With the nudge of the name given to him, he had a vague memory that the doctor had a kid. He'd never paid any attention to her. "She's practicing here?"

"Seems she's covering for her old man, who is on a vacation somewhere south of here. She's staying until after the holidays, then is returning to her real job." James stopped and Ethan didn't give him the satisfaction of asking what her real job was. With a sigh, James finally gave in. "She works at a free clinic in Seattle down by the docks."

"Is that it?"

James shrugged. "That's about it." Then he did an abrupt change in the conversation. "They're having a bachelor party for Joey next Wednesday. In a week. I told them I'd let you know."

A bachelor party? God, who would have thought that Joseph Lawrence would even consider marriage again after the mess that had been his first marriage? It was strange the twists and turns life took. Hell, Joey was getting married, and old Dr. Kelly's kid had walked into his life out of the blue. He chuckled softly to himself.

"What's so funny?" James asked with a raised eyebrow.

Ethan ran a hand over his face, then rested his head back on the leather of the chair support and sighed. "Life."

James didn't ask for any clarification of that one word, but said, "Ring if you need me," before taking off.

Ethan heard his retreating footsteps on the wooden floor, and called out, "Tell Isabel to bring down breakfast in about an hour."

"You've got it, boss." The other man returned. "Any other orders?"

He hesitated, then said, "Find out an address for Dr. Kelly's daughter…so I can send a payment for services rendered."

"Sure thing," James said without bothering to hide the chuckle in his voice at Ethan's choice of words.

MORGAN SAT in her father's office in the old building where he'd practiced medicine on Shelter Island for as long as Morgan could remember. It looked the same—cluttered, worn and comfortable—but now it seemed so small to her. She couldn't remember ever thinking that until she'd come back this time. The huge desk took up most of the space, and sagging shelves of medical books took up the walls. Morgan exhaled and tipped back in the swivel chair, turning it enough to see out the single window to her left.

The building was on the water side of the main street of Shelter Bay, with her dad and mom's house in back. Across the street, there was a series of specialty shops that had sprung up since she'd last been home. The offices had a side view of the bay, but the house had one that came close to being as good as any on the island. Not as spectacular as those views from the Grace estate, but pretty impressive nonetheless.

Her last appointment of the day had left and it was late, almost six o'clock. Rain came down in mists, driven by the wind skimming in over the rough waters of the sound. She'd thought about Ethan Grace off and on during the day and had even considered calling the estate to make sure he was okay. Then she remembered the woman she'd finally found at the main house and her assurances that "Mr. Grace would be well taken care of." That someone called James would take care of everything.

Ethan Grace had a staff and he had money, which was certainly more than she had. She was the lone doctor on the island right now, and as far as money went, if she had enough she would have helped her father update his equipment, and maybe figured out how to start a four-bed clinic that he'd only dreamed of for years on the property next door. There was no hospital on the island, and when a medical emergency came up, patients were transported either by ferry or by helicopter to the mainland. Sometimes that wasn't good enough. Her father, a pure idealist, dreamed of being able to offer decent emergency care. She'd never understood how he could, given the money it would take to build the clinic, but he'd never given up on the idea over the years.

Dreams came easily, but reality with her father was another matter. She'd always known she'd come back here sooner or later to help her father and possibly take over for him. Somewhere in the future, the very distant future. Having the new clinic would be terrific, if it could happen. Until then, they had to make do with what was here, but she knew her father wasn't at all comfortable with the current limitations of his equipment and facilities. She wouldn't have been, either, if she'd had to practice here instead of just visiting.

More staff would have been nice, she thought as she sat forward and reached for the thick stack of mail that had been piling up over the past few days. She sorted through the envelopes, more than aware that quite a few were bills. A couple could have been payments, but a certified letter that Sharon Long, her nurse/receptionist, had signed for that day stopped her. Morgan noted the return address, E.P.G. Corporation, Development and Acquisitions Division, along with a Seattle address that she knew was in the business district. She hesitated before she finally opened it and scanned the correspondence.

It was a very formal letter with *wherefors* and *forthwiths* sprinkled liberally through it. From what she could gather, the lease on the building that housed her father's offices and all other structures wouldn't be renewed in March. Her throat tightened. Their home was included. She was stunned. She'd never known that her father rented the property. He'd built the offices, she thought, or maybe that was just what she'd assumed. Maybe they'd been there when they moved here and he fixed them. She didn't really know; she'd been a baby when he'd opened the offices.

Morgan stared at the letter, but the words didn't change. The E.P.G. Corporation was putting her father out. She knew that he couldn't have known about this before he left last week. If he had, he never would have gone, and he wouldn't have talked about the possibility that the land next to them might be going up for sale in the near future. "We just have to get the money," he'd told her the night before he left. "I have some saved, and I've got a good enough reputation to get a sizable loan, but getting all of the equipment will be hard." He'd grinned at her. "But we'll do it someway or another." Always the optimist, whether reality bore it or not.

Her mother had been the grounded one, and her father the

dreamer. A terrific doctor but still a dreamer. And he'd signed a simple lease for all of this, including their home.

Morgan reached for the phone to call her dad, but drew back suddenly. She couldn't call him and give him the news. He'd barely arrived at the house he'd rented in Arizona for the month. She looked down at the letterhead on the notice, then reached for the phone again and dialed the first number listed.

A very pleasant female voice announced, "You have reached the offices of Development and Acquisitions for the E.P.G. Corporation. Our offices are closed now, but if you know the extension of the party you wish to contact, please enter it now or leave a message after the tone." Morgan hung up and dialed the second number. This time a man answered. "You've reached the main offices of the E.P.G. Corporation. How may I help you."

Morgan tried to explain the contents of the letter, but the man politely but firmly cut her off. "Ma'am, that's a matter for our development and acquisitions department. I can give you their number if you'd like?"

"I have it," she said. "I just need to talk to someone and not a recording about a property on Shelter Island."

"You'll need to call back during office hours and I'm sure that someone can help you then."

"What office is this?"

"Corporate towers, ma'am. And everyone is gone for the day."

"There's no one—?"

"Ma'am, even if Mr. Grace was in town, he'd have left by now."

Mr. Grace? She felt the blood drain from her head and she asked, "Ethan Grace?"

"Yes, ma'am, but he's not here, and even if he was—"

She put the phone down, cutting off his polite response. Ethan Grace. She wasn't sure what the *P* stood for, but now she knew what the *E* and the *G* stood for in the company name. It was his corporation. The Graces owned a lot of the island, she knew that, but she'd never suspected that they owned this place and she'd never known his company's name. Or that the building and home could be pulled out from under them this way.

If she'd known about the letter yesterday, she could have spoken to Ethan when she'd found him half-conscious in his bedroom, but now he was "being taken care of," and there was no way she could go back there again. She stopped that thought. She'd walked onto the beach yesterday without any trouble. She'd gone up the stairs and entered the house without anyone stopping her. If she did it once, she could do it again. And he was the boss, injured or not, over everything.

Speaking directly to him, instead of someone in one of his many corporate divisions, sounded sensible. That was another thing she'd learned at the clinic—the fewer people between you and what you needed, the better everyone was in the end. If she could convince Ethan to renew the lease, her father wouldn't have to know about the notice. If she was incredibly lucky, she might even be able to convince Ethan to sell the complete property to her father, if they could get the money somehow. Besides, it would be bad PR for the company to just shut them down.

She stood and placed the letter back in the envelope. After slipping it into her pants pocket, she braced herself to face Ethan Grace again. The man she'd found last night had been vulnerable and in real pain. And when she saw him again, she knew it would be a different situation completely. He was regarded as a genius in the business world, but he was also known to be hard-hitting, bordering on ruthless and giving no quarter to anyone. Traits, she was sure, he shared with his pirate ancestor. But instead of sailing to the south and pillaging and plundering small settlements, he was headquartered in Seattle and he used, from what she heard, a corporate jet or helicopter to pillage and plunder floundering companies. He would be a formidable match.

A knock sounded on the office door and Sharon peeked inside. Middle-aged, she was dressed in jeans, a T-shirt worn under an open blue smock and tennis shoes. She had a pleasant face and was usually smiling, but this time she looked a bit contrite. "Sorry, I forgot to get this to you," she said as she handed her an envelope.

Morgan took it and looked down at her name scrawled in black ink just under what appeared to be an embossed monogram. "What is it?" she asked.

"Don't know. He just said to give it to you."

"He who?" she asked as she looked up at the other woman.

"The guy who brought it. Don't know him. Never saw him before." She had her jacket over her arm and was obviously in a hurry to get going. "Forty or so, preppy, gray hair and great smile. Drove a huge black SUV with tinted windows."

It didn't sound like anyone Morgan knew, either. "Okay, thanks."

Sharon said what she always did when she left for the day, "Safe trip home," then laughed at her own joke. Morgan lived right behind the building, all of fifty feet from the office.

"Same to you," Morgan responded, not able to muster a laugh this time. Not when she knew that her father could lose that very home—and the offices—within three months.

She turned, looked down at the envelope Sharon had handed to her and tucked her forefinger under the flap to open it. Inside was a folded sheet of paper along with a smaller piece of paper that fell to the floor. Picking it up, she saw it was a check for two hundred dollars. She was stunned to read the person's information in the top left corner.

E.P.G. Corporation. Then she read the accompanying letter. *Thanks for your help. If this isn't sufficient, please bill the address at the top.* The signature was a tangle of letters that she could barely make out, but she had no doubt it belonged to Ethan Grace. He was paying for her services. She suddenly smiled. And he'd just given her the opening she'd been looking for to contact him in person again.

Chapter Three

"Did you give the check to the doctor?" Ethan asked as James came into the makeshift office in the guest house.

James's graying hair was damp from the rain outside, and the shoulders of his beige jacket were dark. "Yeah, it's done."

"Good, good." Ethan pushed back in his chair, careful to keep his bad foot safely resting on the ottoman. "Was it enough?"

"Don't know. I gave it to her receptionist. She said the doctor was in with a patient and that she'd be a while, so I left it with her."

Ethan dropped his pen on the contracts he'd been scanning, and sank back in the leather swivel chair. After sitting at his desk for the better part of the day, his shoulders and injured leg had cramped. He wore shorts because they were easier to put on than long pants, with a plain white shirt he'd left unbuttoned.

"That place is ancient," James said.

"What?"

"The doctor's office. It's in that old building on the sound side of the main street. I don't see how anyone could practice medicine there."

He remembered the property where the doctor had set up his practice after he'd moved it out of his home at the same location. The office, a nondescript building with a flat roof, two large windows in front and parking in front, had been built closer to the street. He'd been in there a couple of times years ago and remembered the tiny rooms, the waiting area with green vinyl chairs and month-old magazines.

"I guess it works for him," he said, wondering why Morgan would have become a doctor, only to come back here to take over her father's practice, such as it was.

"Speaking of doctors," James said. "What did Dr. Perry say when you called him?"

"That I'll live," he murmured.

"Well, does that make us lucky or not?"

Ethan chuckled at that. "Depends on your mood, doesn't it?"

James echoed his laugh. "Well, your mood's good today. Despite the rain and the cold and all the organizers hurrying around in the main house as if they're planning an event for world peace."

"That's why I'm down here." He glanced up. "No, that doesn't mean you can move in, either."

James held out a hand palm out toward Ethan. "Did I ask?"

"You were going to," Ethan said, then swiveled his chair to face the papers on the desk again.

"I was thinking, though, if you had another fall, where would you want me? Up at the house where you have to ring for me or right here to help you up off the floor?"

He remembered the doctor "helping him up," and knew if he had to choose between James and her, the choice was simple. "I'll manage," he said.

"You always do," James conceded. "So what do you want for dinner?"

A red-haired doctor with a gentle, cool touch. The thought stunned him, and he pushed it out of his consciousness. "Surprise me."

"You've got it."

Ethan checked the wall clock. It was almost six. One look out the window showed him the rain was easing, but the wind was gusting off the water. "Bring it down in an hour."

"No problem. What about the bachelor party? Are you in or aren't you?"

He'd barely had time to spend with Joe since his friend had come back, and had only met his fiancée once—she'd given Ethan a quick hug and a thank-you for throwing them the wedding party. He wanted to sit and talk with his friend. "Sure, count me in."

"Great," James said. "I haven't been to a good bachelor party for years."

"Don't count on this one being groundbreaking," Ethan commented and turned back to the contracts.

"I'm easy. Give me a beer and someone coming out of a cake and I'm happy." With that, he left.

When the door finally shut, Ethan knew he couldn't work. He slowly got to his feet and, with the aid of his crutch, made his way back through the house to the French doors. He pushed open the closest one and stepped out onto the deck. The rain was barely a mist now, but the air was still heavy with dampness and a deep chill.

He noticed in passing that the pot he'd broken hadn't been replaced, just removed. He gripped the railing, and looked down at the beach to the south. He didn't realize what he was doing, until he found himself scanning the water's edge in both directions. She wasn't there. No red-haired doctor walking the sands. He was vaguely disappointed, then he chuckled to himself. Who wouldn't be disappointed not to see Morgan Kelly coming toward them?

The wind was stronger now, but he didn't mind it or the cold. Since the accident, he liked the coolness around him.

Heat tended to make him feel suffocated, and worse yet, it made his bad leg throb. Now all that bothered him was that he was here, alone. Maybe he'd call Natalie and see if she could come over for a day or so. But when he thought about it, he found the idea didn't appeal to him for some reason.

Before he could figure out why, he caught movement on the beach to the south, and thought for a moment that he was conjuring up what he wanted to see instead of seeing the reality of an empty beach. Was that really Morgan Kelly coming into view, her brilliant hair loose and wind-tossed around her face? Walking toward him with easy strides, in dark clothes, the sway of her hips hit him hard. She came closer, and he knew she was real. She was there, on the beach heading in his direction.

He watched her, wondering why he felt so pleased that she'd appeared again, then she stopped. She turned and tilted her head and, even at the distance, he felt the impact of her gaze meeting his. Instinctively, he raised his hand in greeting and saw her do the same. He didn't even think twice before cupping his hands to his mouth and shouting down at her, "Come on up!"

She cocked her head to one side, then touched her right ear. He thought he could hear her reply, "What?"

He yelled louder. "Come up!"

This time he knew she heard him and was pleased when she nodded, waved, then started walking toward the bluffs. She was soon out of sight, and he waited. Just when he was starting to think she'd simply vanished, he heard her footsteps hit the wooden treads of the deck steps, then she appeared around the corner of the house.

Her hair was curling furiously around her shoulders, and her makeup-free face showed more than a few freckles. She wore slender jeans, her leather jacket open to show a white shirt tucked into the band at her narrow waist and boots that looked too heavy for her to walk in. The smile she gave him made his heart catch for a moment, then he smiled back. "Another house call?" he asked, wondering why he couldn't just say, "Good to see you again."

She came closer, and he saw her lips were as pale and as full as he remembered, and she probably wasn't more than five foot three or four. She had her hands pushed into the pockets of her jacket and color touched her cheeks from the cold.

"I guess you could call it that," she responded in a voice that was soft yet throaty at the same time. He saw her gaze flick over him before she met his eyes again. "You know, if you run around half-dressed in this weather, it can't be good for you."

He waved aside her comment, saying, "I'm cold-blooded," and was taken back when she flashed a grin so bright it felt as if the sun had just broken through the clouds.

"Like your ancestor?"

He chuckled at that. "No, that old guy was hot-blooded, in the truest sense of the word. He had eight children, two illegitimate, at least that he knew of."

Her smile turned rueful. "Well, that's a fact I hadn't heard before. How about you? Eleven small Graces hiding around here?"

"I told you, I'm cold-blooded."

She shrugged. "I guess so. It's freezing out here."

He motioned with his head toward the open door. "Come on in, and I can get you some hot coffee or something more robust."

"Hot grog?" she asked, the smile growing again.

"If you want it, you've got it."

"I don't even know what it is," she admitted, and he thought he saw a dimple on her left cheek.

"Come on inside and I'll get the recipe."

He wasn't sure what he was doing right then. It was as if he was standing back watching himself flirt with the doctor, and he wasn't at all sure what the other Ethan was doing. Or if he really wanted it to go anywhere. But with her less than a couple of feet from him, he wasn't going to question his actions too much. He liked looking at her, enjoyed her smile and remembered her lying on top of him in bed during their first meeting.

"If you have to cook grog, don't bother. I don't cook."

He motioned to the doors again, and she entered the house. He followed her inside and closed the door behind them. "I don't know if it's cooked or not, but it does sound good on a night like this."

She turned to face him, and for a moment, the overhead light caught her in its soft glow. He felt his stomach tighten. She really was pretty in a simple way with her freckles and the bluest eyes. He would have laughed at that little summation if she hadn't been standing there. Simple? What woman was ever simple? None he'd known.

"Do me a favor and hit the button on the fireplace by the wood cradle."

She headed toward the couches that faced the view outdoors and the huge stone fireplace. He watched her as she stripped off her jacket, laid it on one of the couches, then crossed to crouch in front of the hearth. Her jeans were tighter than he'd thought, and he felt a familiar tightening in his. *It has been a while,* he thought as he sat.

He heard the whoosh as the fire caught, and Morgan stood, watching the leaping flames before she looked at him. "Good?"

He studied her. "Perfect."

She took a seat on the edge of the other couch and clasped her hands on her knees. She'd seemed at ease outside, but now he could sense tension in her. He hoped she didn't think he was being predatory getting her in here or that he had ulterior motives. Okay, maybe he did, but he hoped he wasn't that obvious. *Calm down,* he told himself. *Take a deep breath. Enjoy what you can.* And he smiled at Morgan. "I'm glad you came." That was the truth.

She smiled back and murmured, "So am I."

Good, he told himself. *Very good.*

LAST NIGHT Morgan hadn't had time really to look at Ethan Grace beyond the checkup she gave him. Now she had the chance to see the man who held the fate of her father's whole future in his hands, and to some extent, her own fate. The brown eyes that had been blurred from pain the night before, were now sharp and focused. His dark brown hair was combed straight back from a wide forehead, and his face was all ridges and angles. He had a strong jaw and a nose that surprisingly looked as if it might have been broken at one time.

She had been so relieved to have an excuse to come here and talk to him, but now that she was facing him, her mind was blank. The well-rehearsed words she'd gone over and over on the walk here were gone. "So, the grog," she heard herself saying simply to fill the silence, "is it cooked?"

He frowned slightly. "I'll find out." With that he reached for a phone sitting on a side table to his right and pushed in four numbers. Without preamble, he said, "Find out how you make hot grog." He hung up and looked at her as if to say, "Mission accomplished," but all he said was, "Done."

It was that easy for him—pick up a phone, give an order and know that it will be carried out. An order, such as, "Get Dr. Kelly out of his offices and home by March." That thought gave her focus and got her past the man himself. "I can't say

I've lost sleep at night wondering about hot grog, but just knowing can be a good thing."

"I guess so," he agreed.

She felt her hands start to tingle and knew she was clasping them much too tightly. Deliberately she eased them apart, pressed her palms to her knees and rubbed the rough denim of her jeans. "I came here to…" She cleared her throat and didn't say what she thought she would right then. "To say that I never sent you a bill, so I certainly didn't expect any payment."

"I needed help, and you were there. I owe you for that."

He owed her. This was perfect. Thankfully she didn't call him on it and say, "You owe me my father's office and our home." She shook her head and just said, "I'm glad I could help."

"So am I," he replied.

The phone rang and he picked it up. "Yes?" With the receiver still in his hand, he recited, "Hot coffee, heavy cream, brown sugar, butter, spices. That's it. I guess it's all boiled or brewed or something like that. Do you want some?"

She grimaced. "I'll pass."

"Me, too. How about a brandy or anything else?"

She needed something that would let her relax a bit, but she was worried about drinking anything with alcohol. "I don't know, maybe hot cider," she said.

"Have you had dinner?"

She hadn't thought of food and wasn't at all sure she could eat anything until she got the matter of her father's property settled, but sitting across the table from him would make it easier for her to bring up her request. "No, I haven't."

He picked up the phone again. "Make it dinner for two and add mulled cider and some brandy to the list," he said, then hung up.

Ethan settled again, his injured leg pushed under the coffee table. She frowned at it. "You should have that elevated."

Before he could argue, she stood and grabbed a pillow from the couch. "You paid me two hundred dollars, and that should get you more than what I gave you last night," she said, gently lifting his injured leg to rest the heel of the cast on the pillow, which she'd placed on the coffee table. She went back to her seat, then looked over at him, the table a buffer between them. "How's that?"

"Better."

"Good."

Great conversation, she told herself, and tried to find the words to get started. She glanced at the cast, then figured small talk could lead to big talk, especially if it was about this man. "So, how did that happen?" she asked.

He told her about his accident, and through it all, she sensed his annoyance. She wasn't sure if his frustration was with the driver of the other car for not setting his brake, or with his own driver, who hadn't been available, or with himself for letting it happen. She didn't have to know him well to understand that men like Ethan Grace thought they controlled their lives and everything around them. When they lost control, they hated it.

"Is it a simple fracture?" she asked when he was finished.

"There's nothing simple about it, but that's what the doctor called it."

"Who's your doctor?"

"Maury Perry."

She'd actually heard of the top doctor, but she'd never met him and probably never would. Morgan's patients were regular people with everyday lives and jobs, while Dr. Perry's were well-heeled members of society; their medical worlds weren't apt to collide on any level. "What did he say when he checked you after your fall?"

"'Come to my office and let me charge you an arm and a

leg—your good leg, of course—so I can tell you that you fell and are going to survive.'"

She kept a grin to herself. She'd made fun of the "high and mighty" doctors like Perry more than once, joking about how they charged to say "God bless you" when you sneezed. "And?"

"And I'm here." He waved a hand around the room. "*Stuck* here."

That annoyance was there again. "If you don't like it here, why come?"

"I'm a good patient," he said with a smile that was more like a grimace. "I'm doing what the doctor suggested—take it easy, stay off my foot and definitely not do what I usually do."

"Which is?"

"Work, in a thirty-floor building, take meetings all day, travel on a moment's notice and generally keep things at the office going."

Sensing the road for the conversation was heading right where she wanted it to, she helped it along. "So, is the business collapsing right now because you're here and you aren't wherever it is you prefer to be?"

He threw up his hands in surrender. "I know, I know, I'm not indispensable. Dr. Perry has told me that more than once, and James never lets me forget it."

Before she could ask who James was, the front door opened and the man who, based on Sharon's description, dropped off the check last night, strode into the room with a huge covered tray. "Here you go," he said, and came to put the tray on the table halfway between the two of them.

He didn't look over at her until he removed the cover and was straightening. Then he smiled. "You're the doctor?"

"Yes, Morgan Kelly," she said.

"Dr. Morgan Kelly," he repeated. "I'm James Evans." He

lifted an eyebrow and said, "I heard you tucked him into bed last night."

"I helped him get to the bed," she said.

"Well, I'm grateful, and if there's anything you need, just call on me."

"James," Ethan said, and the man took his time turning from Morgan to his boss. "Where's dinner?"

"Coming. You just ordered it."

Morgan thought that the relationship between the two men had to be more than boss and employee. James didn't seem the least bit fazed by Ethan's commanding tone, not even when he spoke again. "Make sure there's fresh shrimp with it."

"Oh, sure, boss. Fresh shrimp. I'll make a note," he murmured, giving Morgan another grin. "Nice to see you, Doctor."

With that, he left and shut the door behind him. She looked over at Ethan, who was reaching for one of two decanters on the tray. He picked up the one that was steaming and full of rich amber liquid, the mulled cider. The other held brandy. He poured cider into a mug on the tray, and offered it to her. "Your cider," he said. "How about a cinnamon stick?"

Leaning over the table, she plucked a cinnamon stick off the tray and took the cider from Ethan. "Thanks," she replied and resumed her seat.

He ignored the cider for himself and poured a splash of brandy in a snifter before he sat back and looked at her. "Cider ceased being appealing when I was a kid," he said, then smiled. "But brandy? That's different."

"Before dinner?"

"Anytime at all," he murmured.

She cradled the warm mug between both hands, but didn't drink any. Ethan, on the other hand, sipped his brandy, closed his eyes with a sigh and rested the snifter on his thigh. "I needed that," he said. She wasn't aware she'd been frowning at him until he spoke again. "Why are you looking at me as if you're waiting for me to walk off a cliff or, to be more appropriate, to walk the plank?"

"I was wondering if you'd taken any medication today."

He lifted the snifter toward the fireplace and stared at the rich liquid that reflected the flames in the hearth. "Why?"

"Mixing alcohol with those pills could be pretty risky."

He held the glass a moment longer, then put it back down on his thigh. "I took aspirin today. Does that put me at risk?"

She knew her cheeks colored a bit. "Of course not. It's the prescription medication you're taking I'm concerned about—it's very strong."

His dark eyes met hers. "Tell me, could it make a person hallucinate?"

She blinked at the question. "I suppose it could."

"Oh," was all he said before taking another sip of brandy.

She had some of her cider, then settled back in the cushions a bit. She wasn't sure if they'd be alone at dinner, not after James had made his appearance and seemed to do whatever he wanted around Ethan. She'd been ready to get to the point of her visit when the other man had intruded and tried to regroup. "Did Dr. Perry suggest you come here to recuperate?"

"That about sums it up," he muttered.

She bet no one made him do anything he didn't want to do. "They forced you on the ferry and sent you over here into exile?" That brought a crooked grin that transformed his almost harsh face into something that bordered on being boyishly cute. Now that was an odd word to use for a man like Ethan Grace. *Cute.* She quickly covered the smile that twitched on her lips.

"I came by helicopter and no one held a gun to my head, but this does have the flavor of being in exile."

"Then why come?"

"I had other things going on and it made sense."

She didn't push for further details; she wasn't here to learn about his personal or even his business life. She wanted to know about only one thing. "You're the CEO of your company?"

"CEO, COB and any other combination of initials you want to come up with. A real alphabet man."

"Basically you own it."

"The investors and I do."

"But what you say goes?"

"To a point."

"Who do you answer to?"

"The board."

"I mean, do you have an actual boss?"

He frowned at her. "Boss? No, I guess not."

"Then you have the final say on everything your company does?"

He took a drink, then sighed. "In some sense, I guess that's right."

This was it! The opportunity she'd been waiting for. But just as she was about to ask him about the lease, James was back, yelling, "Room service" and crossing the room with another huge tray in his hands. A young woman Morgan thought she'd seen before brought up the rear and headed toward a table by the windows. She cast a sideways glance at Morgan, smiled and kept going. While James came to where they sat, the woman got busy setting the table with linen and crystal. "Just as you asked, boss," James said as he went to the table.

In a matter of minutes everything was laid out. "Dinner is served and the shrimp is exquisitely fresh," James announced.

He didn't have a napkin over his arm, and he didn't bow, but he was as close to being a manservant at that point as anyone could be, except for the obvious sarcasm in his voice. "Thanks," Ethan said and pushed to get up.

James moved quickly, taking Ethan by the arm and helping him off the couch. He let him go when Ethan drew back, clearly wanting to cross to the table himself. Morgan took the chair James held out for her and settled in front of a plate filled with meat and vegetables and a side dish of shrimp all on a pewter charger. The woman poured wine into fine-stemmed goblets, then laid a basket of bread in the middle of the table.

Ethan settled with James hovering over him. "Anything else, sir?"

Ethan looked up and shook his head. "You've done more than enough," he said with a touch of sarcasm, too.

James barked out a laugh, then nodded to Morgan. "Enjoy," he said, then left with the woman and other tray in tow.

Ethan looked at Morgan. "Sorry about that."

"Who is he?" she asked.

He exhaled in a rush. "That's a good question. An assistant, a friend, a thorn in my side and someone I rely on completely and have for the past ten years." He reached for his wine goblet and lifted it in her direction. "Here's to a nice dinner and good conversation…." He glanced over at the closed door before looking back at Morgan. "And to James forgetting his way to the guest house."

She laughed, picked up her own wine and took a small sip of the rich red liquid. As she put her glass down, she met Ethan's dark eyes and he spoke again. "Now, tell me why you came all this way on the beach."

"To see you," she said simply.

His gaze never wavered. "Why?"

She resisted the urge to take another drink of wine and said,

"I have a problem and you're the only one who can fix it for me."

The goblet stopped partway to Ethan's lips, and he stared at her over the rim. "Me?"

"You."

Chapter Four

Ethan forgot about the wine and looked at the woman across the table from him. "What are you talking about?" he asked, entirely certain that her mind was not going down the same road as his. He might have wanted her to visit him again, but not to fix a "problem," at least that's not what he would have called it. Feeling lust for someone wasn't a problem, unless the other person didn't reciprocate.

She drank more wine before her eyes lifted to meet his. He heard her take a breath before she said, "I have something to show you," but she didn't move to show him anything. Instead, she kept speaking in a rush. "You know I was brought up here and lived with my folks in the house behind his office before I left to go to college, then medical school?"

He hadn't thought about that chronology of events, but they made sense. She grew up, left, became a doctor. He nodded and she continued.

"I usually work at a clinic in Seattle, the Wayfarer Medical Care Center." He'd never heard of it. "A month ago, my father called and asked if I'd come home to cover his practice for him while he took a long-needed vacation."

She was a good daughter obviously, and probably a good

doctor, but what did that matter to him? "And?" he asked as he fingered the stem of his wineglass.

"Okay," she said, releasing a breath as if she'd reached a marker that was totally invisible to him. "My father has this idea to expand his facilities on the island to a small four-bed clinic for emergencies and light surgery, so he could give the islanders more than general medical aid. Right now he doesn't have the space or the equipment and has to pack them off to the mainland, or order a helicopter for emergencies. But if he had the extra room, it would be terrific." She paused, staring at him as if he could follow what she was talking about. He didn't.

"And?" he repeated.

She frowned, and he had the oddest feeling that he hadn't understood the way she'd hoped he would. She reached into the pocket of her jeans and extracted a folded envelope. "*And* this." Honestly, he was more interested in the way high color touched her cheeks as she spoke and the brush of freckles across her nose than anything she had said or had in her hand.

He reached for her offering, looked down at it and was taken aback to see an envelope with his company logo on it. The address was on the island, her father's medical offices.

"Go ahead and read it," she said.

He opened the envelope and took out a letter written on his corporate stationery. He skimmed the contents and recognized a formal "quit" notice for the property on the main street. Whatever lease agreement there had been with his company for use of the land and property was being terminated.

"Why are you showing me this?" he asked as he looked at her.

"It's your company," she said, leaning toward him, her dinner totally untouched. "You're taking the property back. You're canceling the lease. You're putting my family out of their home and the medical offices. You'd be closing the only doctor's office on Shelter Island." She bit her lip before adding, "My dad's lived there for thirty years, and my mom did until she passed away ten years ago. I never knew the land and buildings weren't his, but I'm positive they were never late on the rent. My father is a man of his word."

Ethan sat back. "I never said he wasn't."

She flashed a glance at the paper still in his hands, then looked back at him, the earnestness in her expression deepening the color in her cheeks. "Why are you doing this, then?"

He felt as if he'd been blindsided. She had been on the beach, walking, he'd called her up, they'd sat down to dinner. God knew what he'd hoped might happen when he'd invited her in for a drink, but it sure wasn't sitting here talking business and being forced to explain anything to her. "I'm not. This is from our acquisitions and development division, and I don't have a thing to do with it."

She sat there silent for what seemed an eternity, but he didn't miss the look of displeasure on her face. *Wrong answer,* he told himself. *Really wrong.*

"But you *are* the head of the company. It's *your* company. What you say goes."

"That's a simplistic view of the situation," he said as he pushed the letter back in the envelope. "I don't do day-to-day work on the front lines. It's called delegating. The divisions in the corporation run their business, and as long as they don't lose money, I don't interfere."

She sank back in her chair, her expression puzzled. "So you don't have control of your own company?"

"I didn't say that."

"You said—"

"I know what I told you," he said, a bit shocked that his irritation was starting to displace some of the good feelings he'd had since she'd shown up on the beach. "What do you think I can do to fix your problem?"

"Can you stop this eviction?"

"I don't think so," he said, surprised by the touch of bitterness in his voice.

"Then I want you to sell me that property and the one adjacent to it."

The bitterness deepened. It was becoming clear her visit today had been about business, all business. That was probably why she'd smiled when she'd spotted him outside and why she'd agreed to dinner. He wasn't vain enough to think every woman wanted him, but he thought he read people a hell of a lot better than he'd read this woman. She'd likely come by when she'd found him after the fall and been disappointed that he'd been too out of it to talk about the lease. He just bet she'd been annoyed at that. "Talk to acquisitions and development." He tossed the envelope onto the table next to her plate. "Talk to a man named Jaye Fleming. He'll have all the answers for you."

She didn't move to pick it up. "I was hoping you could look into it for me and give me a figure."

His appetite was completely gone now. He pushed the plate away and downed the last of his wine before he spoke again. "A and D sent that to you for one of two reasons—nonpayment on the contract, or they aren't going to renew the option on the lease because they have development plans for the property. Since you think your father wasn't in arrears on his payments, my best guess is the land is slated for development."

"What development?"

He shrugged. "I don't know."

She exhaled in frustration. "But you own the company."

"We've already established that and how it works."

"But you—"

"I let my subordinates run their divisions," he said, cutting off what he knew she was going to say. "If A and D wants that land, they're going to develop it."

"For what?"

"I don't know."

She looked as exasperated as he felt. "Can't you find out?"

He could make one call and ask, but he found he didn't want to. "Call them yourself and ask for Jaye Fleming. He'll know all the ins and outs of the situation. A hell of a lot more than I do." He crossed his arms over his chest, knowing he looked defensive. He didn't care. He was suddenly very tired and his leg was starting to throb. "He should be in the office at nine in the morning."

"Okay," she muttered. "I'll call him. Maybe *he'll* understand that they're taking away our home and the only medical center on the island."

"Maybe he will," he said, and he actually hoped Fleming could say something to make her understand their side of it.

She reached for the envelope. "Thanks." He really wished that she would smile again. But she didn't. "Can you let him know I'll be calling him at nine?"

"Sure. What about dinner?" he asked, motioning to the untouched food.

She didn't even glance at the plate. "I'm not very hungry anymore."

He knew this was over, whatever "this" had been at the start, and the sooner she left, the better. But that didn't stop him from asking, "Are you sure?"

She nodded and stood, then crossed to the couch to get her jacket. "Yes, I'm sure," she said as she slipped on her coat and tugged at her cuffs.

"Do you need a ride back to your place?"

She shook her head and met his gaze. "No, I'll just go back the way I came."

"It's dark," he said, pointing out the obvious.

"I've walked these beaches all my life."

He didn't know what else to say so kept quiet and stayed where he was as she turned and headed for the French doors. She slipped through them without a backward glance, and he released a breath he hadn't been aware he'd been holding. He sat there, listening to her footsteps as she made her way across the deck and down the steps. Finally, he could no longer hear her. He was alone. He looked around the empty house and hated the silence.

"Damn it all," he muttered and turned abruptly to get up, forgetting momentarily about his leg. His foot lurched and a sharp pain shot up into his hip. He waited for the ache to subside to a dull throb before he carefully got to his feet and made his way back to the couch.

When he sank down onto the cushions, there was no brilliant-haired doctor facing him across the low coffee table. So he reached for the brandy, filled his snifter and took a long swallow. The next thing he did was pick up the phone and punch in Natalie's cell number. It rang four times before the call was transferred to her voice mail. "It's Ethan. Just wondering how you're doing." Then he hung up, drained his brandy and poured more.

Morgan Kelly had come here to get the property, to have him sell it to her. Business. He suddenly hated business, but that didn't stop him from making another call. He knew he would wake Fleming, the head of development at E.P.G., and he didn't care. He asked the slightly groggy man about the property and listened as Jaye suddenly become almost animated as he explained the details to Ethan.

The department had gone through their long-term holdings, looking for areas to upgrade and increase the income the company earned on them. One of his men had hit on Dr. Kelly's lease. When they'd looked into it, they'd realized the properties on both sides were theirs, as well. The rent from the doctor's office and house was fair for what it was, but after additional research they'd realized they were sitting on a gold mine. The property's prime view over the sound, its close proximity to the ferry landing and the additional land next door was perfect for a bed-and-breakfast, restaurants on the bluffs, small shops and an island museum. The complex would cater to upscale visitors and feed off their fascination with the island's pirate history.

Ethan asked what he thought the land, as it stood, would sell for on the open market. Jaye spoke up quickly, saying it was invaluable, but Ethan pressed for a price. When he finally got it, the figure even shocked him. Developing the plot was a smart idea. He could literally hear the man sigh with relief when he told him it sounded great.

"A woman named Morgan Kelly will be calling you to-morrow morning about the property," Ethan said. Before Fleming could reply, Ethan added, "Explain the development plans to her, tell her what you told me about the unimproved value and anything else she asks." He hesitated, a bit surprised to realize he was about to say, "Break it all to her gently." Instead he said, "Just make her understand that it's not for sale and won't be."

Fleming agreed without asking any questions. Ethan hung up, had another brandy and stared into the fire. Unless Morgan Kelly was fabulously wealthy, he knew she didn't stand a chance of keeping the property…even if it were for sale.

"Too bad," he said softly to himself and meant it. But that didn't mean anything would change. The deal was a good one for E.P.G., and despite what Morgan thought, about him being the boss, he didn't just wave a hand and lay down edicts. He answered to the board of directors and, from what Fleming had told him, the board was behind this decision completely. Very excited about the possibilities, in fact. Ethan had no desire to argue with the board. No, a Grace had never undermined the corporation and he wouldn't be the first. Even if it meant Morgan Kelly might never smile at him again.

MORGAN WOKE the next morning with a sense of impending doom, then realized it came from what she had planned for the day. The sense of doom only deepened when the receptionist at E.P.G. Corporation's acquisitions and development division told her that Mr. Fleming wasn't in today. He wasn't expected in for the rest of the week. Determined to know what was happening with the property, Morgan found herself talking to another cement wall of a receptionist who, after Morgan had outlined the reason for her call, had said, "I'll check." She came back after putting Morgan on hold for a good ten minutes only to say quickly, "There are no plans to liquidate that property." Before Morgan could say another thing, the woman cut her off with, "I have a call on another line. Have a nice day," and the phone went dead in her ear.

After staring at the receiver in disgust, she slowly got up and padded barefoot through the house to her bedroom, then stripped off her nightgown and stepped into the shower. As the warm water washed over her, she thought that either Ethan hadn't contacted Fleming as he promised, or Fleming was avoiding her. Short of storming the offices in Seattle demanding to speak to Mr. Fleming to get a price for the land, she was stuck dealing with Ethan Grace. She couldn't leave the island until her father was back, and by then it would be too late. Ethan was here. So was she. He was her only chance, although she could admit to herself that her chances with him were almost nonexistent. But if she could just figure out a better way to approach him than she had last night, she still might save her clinic and her home.

She lifted her face to the warm spray. She'd have to figure out how to "play" the man's game, to read his moods, to get his attention—and ultimately his cooperation—and keep it. It was the same dance she did with her patients, the difficult ones who fought her at every step. She'd learn how to approach them, to get through to them and, in the end, get them to do what she knew was best for them. She stepped out of the shower stall and reached for a towel. The only difference this time was she was getting him to do what was best for her.

Morgan thought about little else all day, and once the last patient left the office, she had another plan in place. She'd try to contact Ethan again, but this time she wouldn't take the direct route at all. She'd back off, talk to him, get to know him a bit and, when she had the opportunity, then she'd go in for the strike. She wouldn't take no for an answer. She'd stay until she got a price and made an offer or until he threw her out.

She locked up the offices, walked out the back and stopped before going in the house. It was an old and rambling building, with two stories under a wooden shingle roof that pitched high in the middle. The wraparound veranda and clapboard siding had been painted pale blue for as long as she could remember. The idea they could lose it made her eyes burn with tears. She never cried, but the possibility that this could all be torn down as if it had never existed was devastating. Why hadn't her father ever thought of that? In thirty years, why hadn't he tried to purchase it? She'd always known he was a dreamer, thinking the best of everyone, but she'd never thought he was a lousy businessman.

She went up the steps and inside. She hadn't done a thing for Christmas so far. No tree, no lights, no garlands, no pinecones in the fireplace, but she would, she decided as she hurried through the silent rooms and up the stairs to the room she'd had for forever. Tinsel, lights and a tree. Maybe lights outside, too. She'd do it after she got back.

She quickly changed, dressing in brown corduroy slacks, a bulky knit white sweater and suede boots. She grabbed her leather jacket and went back out into the chill of early evening.

She'd decided to do a frontal approach this time, not a beach approach. She'd drive up to the gate, ring, say she needed to talk to Ethan and hope against hope that he wouldn't turn her away. He'd paid her far too much for her services, and her story was she wanted to return his check. It seemed realistic to her, and she just hoped it would at least get her near him again.

She drove through town, under Christmas lights draped across the street from light post to light post, past shops and stores decorated for the holidays. She went north out of town, and when she got near the Grace estate, well past the old lighthouse, she did what she'd never done before—she turned onto the cobbled drive that led up to the twin wrought-iron gates that barred entry to the sprawling property. She stopped by a call pad and pressed One for the main house as instructed. Almost immediately, a woman's voice came on the line. Morgan gave her name, adding that she was there to see Mr. Grace. There was no hesitation before the voice said firmly, "He's not accepting visitors." With a click, the line went dead.

She sank back in the seat and gripped the steering wheel. Okay, that was only the first try. She wasn't giving up. She reached to press the keypad again, but stopped when she saw a Deliveries sign with an arrow pointing up a side driveway. She revised her plan and backed up to turn onto the road that went along the high fence to another entrance. She stopped the car at a more utilitarian gate, but one that was just as secure as the main gate.

She sat in her old compact car trying to decide what to do next when, miraculously, the gate slid open silently. The next moment, bright lights flashed in her eyes and a horn sounded. A truck was coming out, and she quickly moved to the right to allow it to pass. She couldn't see who was driving, but a sign on the side read something about "rentals." It passed her, then headed away from the estate. She looked up and the gate was still open. She didn't think twice about driving through onto the estate.

She drove onto a cemented area that was separated from the rest of the grounds by high shrubs on both sides. Straight ahead were several parking spots, two already occupied by vans, and another by a car about the same age as hers. She parked beside the old sedan, then got out and turned, barely avoiding a collision with a man rushing past her with his hands full of boxes labeled Linens.

"What are you here for?" he said.

"Silverware," she improvised quickly, even though her hands were empty except for her car keys.

"They're probably waiting," he muttered before he nodded toward an open door at the top of a wooden ramp. "Go on inside and find Roz Quinlan—tall, thin and loud. She'll tell you what to do, and love doing it." He started off, calling over his shoulder, "Good luck."

She wasn't interested in Roz Quinlan, just Ethan Grace. Following his directions, she found herself in what looked like a huge storage area. Plain white plaster walls were lined with metal shelves full to sagging with cleaning supplies and unmarked boxes.

"I said *simple!*" A woman's voice that was as clear as if

she'd been shouting right next to Morgan came through an arched stone doorway. "Do it now."

Morgan headed toward the sound, walking into a massive kitchen with worn stone walls and a heavily beamed ceiling. The room may have looked rustic, but the appliances were all high-tech and stainless steel with enough supplies and storage space for an army.

She saw the woman she bet was Roz. At about six feet, she definitely was tall but more willowy than thin, and she was dressed all in red from her leggings to her tunic. As if she sensed Morgan there, she turned to her as soon as she entered the kitchen.

"Mistletoe?" she asked, as she strode over to her.

"Excuse me?"

"Wen Day Suppliers? Mistletoe? You're Ms. Wong?"

Morgan barely stopped her laugh. She doubted she looked like any Ms. Wong, but you never knew. "No, I'm sorry, I'm Dr. Kelly. I'm here to see Mr. Grace."

Her eyes widened a bit. "Doctor? Is there an emergency?"

"Oh, not a medical emergency, no."

She exhaled heavily. "Thank goodness." A woman dressed in a sweatsuit with a huge Santa head embroidered on the top, ran into the kitchen. "Miss Quinlan, they need you to check on positioning for the florist."

Roz turned and spoke with undisguised exasperation, "It's Ms. Quinlan, and it's about time. I'll be right there."

Roz glanced back at Morgan. "Gotta go," she said, and headed after the other woman.

Morgan wished she'd asked Roz how to find her way to the guest house, but shouldn't have worried about it. Right then an older lady dressed all in navy came through a side door, spotted Morgan and inclined her head. "May I help you?" Her graying hair had been cut short and framed a pleasant if plain face and, with a subdued, almost serene manner, put her in direct contrast to Roz.

"I was just…" Morgan knew telling her the truth was out of the question unless she wanted to be escorted away before she even got to see Ethan. "Roz—Ms. Quinlan—she asked me to check on…" She tried to think, then came up with the perfect answer. "The lighting on the back terrace."

"Oh," she said, and Morgan could tell from that one word this woman was not going to refuse Roz anything. She pointed to a closed door to Morgan's left. "Either go through the ballroom or go down the hallway, out the greenhouse door, then to your right."

"Thank you," she said.

The woman nodded, but didn't leave. She was waiting for Morgan to get out of the kitchen, and she obliged. She crossed to the door, went into an arched corridor fashioned from stone. Her feet struck the hard flooring, the sound echoing around her as she went along the hall, turned a corner and found herself at a heavy, windowless door. She pulled it open and walked into the greenhouse. Plants were everywhere and near the back of the space was a cluster of small tables and a few chaise lounges. The air was humid, at least eighty degrees, but through the foggy glass, she could see the terrace. More importantly, she caught sight of the guest house in the distance.

She hurried past the tables and stepped out into a chill that was all the more jarring after the warmth in the greenhouse. She turned from the terrace and made her way across the grass to the smaller house on the bluffs.

For the first time she went to the main entry. She lifted her hand to knock, ready to speak to Ethan about her father's situation, but only hit air when the door abruptly opened without warning. A woman holding a stack of folders in her hand blocked the way. She was obviously surprised at Morgan's appearance, but hid it quickly with a polite smile. "Can I help you?"

"Hello," she said. "I don't mean to intrude, but is Mr. Grace available? I'm Dr. Kelly."

"Let me check," she said, then turned, but Ethan was already coming up behind her. "Dr. Kelly, sir."

"Dr. Kelly," he said. "Hello."

The woman looked from Morgan to Ethan, then left with her load of files. Wearing khaki shorts and a white shirt that was entirely unbuttoned and showing more than a bit of a strong-looking chest, Ethan looked incredibly comfortable and relaxed. His good foot was bare, and he leaned on a single crutch for balance. She exhaled and when she spoke, she didn't say what she'd rehearsed in the car. Instead, she blurted, "I came to apologize."

He moved a step closer. "For what?"

"For acting so rudely last night," she said.

He studied her for a long moment, and she could only imagine what he was thinking. His face was neutral until he motioned her inside. "Come on in," he said, "and we'll talk about it."

She took him up on his offer, and once she was inside, he reached with the crutch to push the door shut while his gaze flicked over her. "Did you walk up the beach?"

"No," she said, heading into the living area. "I drove."

She heard his cast sliding across the hardwood floor as he came up behind her, then a deep sigh. She turned and he was on the couch, looking up at her. "Please, sit down," he said as he rubbed a hand on the nape of his neck. "You're giving me a pain in the neck looking all the way up at you."

He smiled; she couldn't. She quickly sat down, finding

herself in the same position she'd taken the night before and she was just as nervous. "How's your leg?" she asked.

He tapped his knee just above the cast. "Bearable."

"You're on it too much," she said.

"Probably." He studied her from under narrowed lids. "Did you call my offices?"

She nodded. "This morning."

"And?"

She sighed. "Mr. Fleming wasn't in and won't be for a while, but I was told that there are no plans to sell the property."

He frowned. "Fleming wasn't there?"

"That's what the woman said."

"And?"

"Why do you do that?" she asked, digging her nails into her palms, her nerves raw.

"Do what?"

"Say 'And?' as if you're politely asking a question when, in fact, you're trying to drag information out of me."

He blinked at her as if that question took him aback. "I guess it comes from doing business. You need to get as much information as you can from the other side to find out what you need to know. Encourage them to talk while you say as little as possible."

A less-than-subtle method of intimidation and control. "But we aren't in any sort of business negotiations. You made that completely clear last night. At least, it's not your direct business."

He raised his hands slightly, palms out to her. "Sorry." He didn't sound particularly sorry at all.

"Sure," she said, not saying any of the words she'd rehearsed on the way here. Instead, she restated the impulsive apology she'd made when he'd come to the door. "As I said, I came to apologize…for leaving the way I did, and not even touching the dinner you ordered. It was inexcusable and rude."

He smiled crookedly at her words. "Inexcusable? Hardly. *Inexcusable* would have been if you threw the food at me, dish and all, then stormed out. You were quite civilized."

He was giving her a break, making a joke, and she grabbed at it as if it were a lifeline. She chuckled, but it sounded tight to her. "I never throw good food at people, and storming out takes too much energy."

The smile stayed at the corners of his lips. "That's a relief," he said.

She dove in headfirst. "Can we start again?"

"Why not?" He actually looked relieved that she didn't seem to be here to go after him about the land again.

Be patient, she told herself. She had two weeks before her father came back. Two whole weeks. No point in pushing Ethan if it was going to get her anywhere. "Good," she lied, hoping he'd stop her. "That's all I came for. Now, I should be going."

"If we're starting again, why don't we give dinner another try tonight?"

She hesitated, but not because she had to think twice about his offer—it was perfect. Before she could respond, though, he pushed himself to his feet and came over to her without the aid of his crutch. He held out his hand to her. "I'm Ethan Grace."

Chapter Five

Ethan seldom let emotions interfere with business negotiations, but when Morgan agreed to have dinner with him, he felt an inordinate amount of relief. He took her hand in his, feeling her heat and the touch of her slender fingers in her light grip.

"Morgan Kelly," she said softly.

"Nice to meet you," he said, and made himself let go of her hand. "Would you like to start the evening right now? It's not fashionably late yet, but it is getting pretty dark."

She seemed to think about it, and her hesitation made him tense for a moment before she nodded. "Okay, sure."

"Great," he said, and went back to his seat. He watched her do the same, all the while worrying the leather. He tried to remember the last time he'd wanted a woman to stay with him as much as he wanted Morgan Kelly to stick around right then. "Any aversions to food?"

She shrugged out of her jacket and spoke as she laid it on the arm of the sofa by her. "I'm not fond of sour cream, artichokes or sweet potatoes, but anything else is fine."

He felt a smile on his lips that came so very easily. "Okay, no artichokes or sweet potatoes covered with sour cream."

He hoped she'd return his grin, but he wasn't that lucky. She turned from him and reached into the pocket of her jacket as she spoke. "That about covers it." Then she held up her cell phone. "Sorry, but I have to make sure I hear it."

"Can't you have someone else cover for you?"

That did bring a touch of a smile, but it was more wry than humorous. "I'm the only doctor on the island right now, and Sharon, my nurse, can only do so much for the patients."

"I guess you can't turn the phone off, then?"

"It's a tempting thought, but no, I can't."

He liked sitting there just talking, hoping to find out more about her, but their conversation was interrupted when the house phone rang. He held up a finger to Morgan, then reached for the receiver.

"You're going to have a visitor any minute," James said without waiting for Ethan's greeting.

He didn't bother to ask how James knew about Morgan; James knew everything. "You're too late. She's already here, and I was just about to call the kitchen to bring us dinner."

"She's there?" James asked, sounding as if Ethan had told him he'd grown a second head. "There with you? Now?"

"Yeah. Put in an order for poached salmon, salad and vegetables—except sweet potatoes or artichokes. Dig out a nice wine, too."

"And some privacy?" James asked.

"Smart man," Ethan murmured, then hung up. "I take it you went through the house this time?"

"Yes, I did."

He laced his fingers loosely over the cotton of his shirt. "I guess most house calls come through the front door?"

"In general, yes, but I don't usually make house calls to a castle, especially not to one built by an infamous pirate."

"Oh, the house wasn't built by the old guy."

A frown touched her expression. "I always heard it was. At least, I think that's what I was told."

"He built his house here, and from what we know, it was something like a castle and huge. But that structure was leveled over a hundred years ago by a storm that almost blew the island out of the water."

Her frown faded. "Oh, sure, I remember hearing about the big storm of 1904. My great-great-grandfather was a merchant seaman. He came here after to help rebuild the town, then stayed. I never knew that Bartholomew's castle was a casualty, though."

"The stones crumbled and ceilings fell, two turrets were wiped out, four of the six fireplaces bit the dust and no one lived here for about twenty years after that. Finally my grandfather decided that a house on the island would be a good investment in the family's future and rebuilt on the site, using as much of the original stone as he could."

Her face softened in a way that only enhanced her attractiveness. "I like that, using the old stones, rebuilding on the same spot. I just can't figure out how I've never heard the story."

He lowered his voice to the level of mock conspiracy. "We Graces never broadcast our vulnerabilities. That's a lesson that Bartholomew passed down—never let your enemy know when you're less than at your strongest."

"That's a very good lesson for business—to never let your opponent see what's getting to you, or know what can ruin you."

He wasn't sure how this conversation got around to business strategies, but he didn't like it as much as talking about her. "Never let them see you sweat," he said.

The door opened abruptly, and James strode into the house carrying a bottle of wine and two goblets in his hands. "Boss, I brought this down so you can…" His voice trailed off as he caught the sight of Morgan out of the corner of his eye. He turned to her, looked back at Ethan, then tried to cover the surprise Ethan could see so clearly on his face with a smile for Morgan. "Good evening, Dr. Kelly."

"Call me Morgan, please."

"Morgan," he repeated, and looked in the direction of the bedroom. He glanced back at Ethan. "Is there a problem?"

"With what?"

"Your leg?" James asked. He seemed to be deliberately keeping his back to Morgan. His eyebrows were drawn together over his eyes in an almost straight line.

"Except for being in this damn cast? No." What was James's problem?

"Then why is the doctor here?"

"To see me," he said slowly, as if talking to a small child. "We're going to have dinner and some of that wine, if you ever let go of it."

"But I thought…" James appeared truly puzzled about something, then finally said, "You do know you have company on their way down here…any minute now?"

Ethan frowned. "What are you talking about?"

"That matter in Paris?" he said obscurely. "The *problem* with transportation and timing?" Suddenly Ethan understood, and James knew the moment he did. *Natalie.* "Well, you'll need to deal with it right away, if not sooner."

Ethan sat a bit straighter. "Here and now?"

"Absolutely." He finally put the goblets and wine on the table and gave Ethan one last look, obviously waiting for him to give him an order, any order before he asked, "Anything else?"

Ethan had called Natalie Reins but hadn't reached her, and a part of him hadn't been all that disappointed. Now she was coming here to see him? Why? She hadn't called to say she'd be arriving early. He realized he wished she'd called so he could have told her *not* to come. His reaction certainly told him that whatever he'd thought was between the two of them was superficial at best and self-serving at worst.

He glanced at Morgan, who was patiently waiting for the

two men to finish, and he decided to tell James to intercept Natalie, to tell her any lie he could come up with to get her to leave. But if she came all this way, Ethan's refusal to see her would bring on an explosion of major proportions. One thing he'd learned during their six-month relationship was that Natalie was not easily ignored. It hadn't mattered before. Now it did. He sighed, turning from Morgan's inquiring expression. "Okay," he said. "Try to give me a bit of time?"

James hesitated. "If I can figure out where it went to," he said, then with a quick "Good evening" to Morgan, he left.

Ethan looked at Morgan. "I'm sorry," he said and he was. "I've got—"

"Business from Paris to take care of," she supplied as she stood. When he shifted to get up, she motioned him to stay put. "No, rest up for your business," she said with an expression he couldn't read. He was almost certain that the words *rest up for business* weren't intended as a double entendre, but that didn't stop him from avoiding her gaze.

"This was unexpected," he said as he stared at the cast on his leg. "Very unexpected."

"No problem." He looked back at her as she shrugged into the jacket she'd been wearing, then flipped her hair over the collar. "Nine-to-five doesn't always apply to business." She finally smiled, a slow grin that touched her eyes as she pushed her cell phone back into her jacket pocket. "Just ask any doctor."

"It's not that bad for me," he said.

The smile lingered on her full lips. "It's not that bad for me, either. Not anymore. Certainly not like my internship." She grimaced. "Now that's social and sleep deprivation to the extreme."

"I can only imagine," he said.

She hesitated, ready to go, then motioned to his damaged leg. "Make sure you keep it elevated."

"Sure thing," he said and grabbed at a pillow off the back of the couch, but she moved more quickly and had the pillow before he did. She bent over him, lifting his leg with one hand and, placing the pillow on the coffee table with the other, rested his cast upon it. Then she smiled again, and his regret that she was leaving only deepened.

The expression lit her blue eyes for a fleeting moment. "No charge," she said, then headed for the door, taking that smile with her.

She got to the door before he called out after her, "Thanks for coming. Sorry about dinner."

"Don't worry about it," she said, then she was gone.

He watched the closed door for a long moment, wishing it would open again, that she'd come back, saying she was going to stay. The second part of that wish was for Natalie to have to jet back to Paris right away. But both wishes were shattered when there was a knock at the door right before it swung open and Natalie was there, dressed all in black, her blond-white hair windblown. From the look on her face, she'd passed Morgan on her way out. There wasn't anger or even curiosity, just a look that seemed to say, "Now that I'm here, you don't need her."

He tried to smile, wondering why it had never been this hard to show pleasure at seeing her before. "Natalie. What a surprise."

"Oh, Ethan," she said in her breathless voice and, making a beeline for him, tossed her purse on the couch where Morgan had sat just moments ago. She was a cloud of hot perfume and soft femininity that encompassed him as she sank into his lap. He took her kisses and fought a sense of suffocation until she moved back and he gasped at the pain that shot up his leg.

"Ouch!"

She stood immediately, but didn't give him much room at all. She was looking down at him, the diamonds and rubies almost flashing on her fingers. "Sorry, baby, I forgot for a minute."

She didn't give him a chance to respond before she went to check out the guest house, then swung back toward him, letting her silky hair swirl around her shoulders, so pale against the black of her sweater.

"My God, confined to this tiny guest house," she said with a click of her tongue. "How the mighty have fallen." She grinned and spread her arms to him. "But I'm here, with more than a touch of jet lag, to cheer you up and to play doctor." She grinned suggestively, totally unaware that her words made him wish someone else were "playing doctor." She stepped over his leg, and sat down next to him, twining her arm with his before she laid her head on his chest. "I need to leave tomorrow at four." She pressed a hand to his bare stomach as she looked up into his face. "Let's not waste time."

He wondered if it was the medication affecting him because here was Natalie, willing and more than able to give him the diversion he'd craved just a day ago, yet he wasn't interested anymore. "I didn't expect to see you," he said as he gently eased her away from him.

She scrunched up her nose. "Oh, Ethan, come on. You've always liked surprises before." She shifted and touched his cast. "And I've never made love to a man in a cast."

He wasn't sure where his next question came from or why it sounded so sarcastic, even to him. "Oh, come on. Never?"

He could tell he'd struck a nerve. She pushed away from him, but didn't get off the couch. Instead, she reached for the wineglass that had been intended for Morgan and pulled the silver corker out of the bottle to pour herself a generous portion. She took a deep drink, then cradling the goblet in both hands, she cast him a shadowed sideways look. "Who've you been talking to, Ethan?"

"What?"

"Okay, okay," she said, shrugging dramatically, causing one of her diamonds to sparkle wickedly in the overhead light. "There was one time, oh, maybe two years ago, long before you and I... Well, I was in Switzerland, and my skiing instructor, he—" She shrugged again, then took another drink before going on. "His name was Eric, and I felt sorry for him. He took an awful fall and broke his ankle, and he was miserable." She bit her lip. "It was terrible, and I felt so badly because he was showing me how to ski and he got tangled up in a root, and—" She shrugged once more. "I just felt responsible in some way."

"So you played doctor?" he asked.

She turned to him. "I tried to help him."

The idea of her and some poor ski instructor with a cast, was too much for him and he laughed. "I bet you did your best," he managed to say.

"It's not funny," she said with more than a bit of a pout. "He was hurt, and..." She frowned. "You aren't jealous?"

"Jealous?" His smile was definitely gone now. It had never occurred to him to be jealous of anything Natalie did. "Of course not."

Now she looked disappointed, and he realized he'd never thought much about Natalie with other men. In fact, it didn't matter to him in the least. "Oh," she said and came closer to him, her voice growing lower now. "I admit I get jealous from time to time."

"Of what?"

She finished her wine and shifted to put the glass on the coffee table before she moved toward him, curling into his side like a kitten. "That woman who left...?"

"Dr. Kelly," he said.

She sat up to look right at him, then smiled with such obvious relief that it almost made him laugh again. "She's a doctor?" He nodded and she sighed. "Well, imagine that."

"Yeah, imagine that," he echoed.

The front door opened and James entered. "Boss," he said as he crossed to where they sat, "there's a problem."

Natalie was business savvy and didn't bother to ask what was going on. Instead, she reached for more wine, got off the couch and carried her drink over to the windows in the back to look out at the night.

James came closer and crouched by the side of the couch to speak to Ethan. "Is this what you want?" he said in a low voice as he nodded toward Natalie.

Ethan closed his eyes, feeling very tired all of a sudden. "No, it's not."

"Lead and I'll follow," James said without hesitation.

"Natalie?" Ethan called over his shoulder.

She came back to stand by James. "What's going on?"

"A mess, and I have to take care of it. Unfortunately, I won't have time for anything else."

She hesitated, then answered the way he thought she would. "Okay," she said. "It's your call. I'll get lost for a few hours. I would really love to take a long hot bath, and—"

"It's not going to be that simple. This will take long hours, maybe a few days, and you said you couldn't stay past tomorrow. I'm sorry, if I'd known you were coming, or if this hadn't happened…" His voice died out because there wasn't anything polite he could say. If she'd called to say she was coming before Morgan had shown up at his door, what would he have said? He didn't know. "I'm sorry."

"Me, too," she said, then looked at James. "Get me to the ferry."

"It doesn't run again until early morning." Before Ethan could reply, James continued. "But I can call Scooter, if the helicopter's available?" He met Ethan's gaze. "Is that okay with you?"

More than okay. "Perfect."

Natalie crossed to get her purse. When she turned, clutching it to her middle, her eyes met Ethan's. She gave him what he felt certain she thought was a seductive look and spoke softly to him, not caring that James was still there. "Can you survive? I can't get back until the wedding."

James was standing slightly behind Natalie, and as she spoke he gave Ethan a look that told him he had to be a fool to send the woman away. "I'll try to survive," Ethan said.

Natalie came to him, bent to kiss him, then drew back. "Remember where we left off," she whispered.

"I'll meet you at the house," James said to her. "I need to contact Scooter about your ride."

"Okay," she said, giving Ethan one more look before she left.

James waited for the door to close then said, "Are you crazy? You've been complaining about being alone and frustrated, then you get a huge gift dropped on your doorstep and you send it back where it came from?"

Ethan squinted up at him. "Why did you come back down?"

"I saw that look in your eyes when you realized Natalie was coming. It wasn't one of happiness."

"When you're right, you're right," he muttered. "Make sure she has everything she needs, and get Scooter here as quickly as you can."

James glanced out the back doors, then at Ethan. "I think he can make a trip. No fog yet, at least nothing heavy."

Ethan checked the time and thought briefly of calling Morgan to see if she was still available for dinner. But the moment had passed for now. "Go and take care of Natalie," he told James.

When the man left, Ethan looked around the room. He was alone again. "Great," he muttered.

By the time he heard the throbbing rotors of the helicopter passing overhead, he was lying in bed, and still very much alone, wondering what he'd been thinking asking Natalie to leave. He second-guessed himself until he closed his eyes and images of Morgan in bed with him flashed through his mind of when she'd helped him. Her body over his, her touch on him.

Now he wondered what he'd been thinking to let Morgan leave.

MORGAN HAD RETURNED to her parents' house and had been on the phone ever since. Her cell had rung as she drove out of the gates of the Grace estate, her service calling with a non-emergency. By the time she got home and was sitting in the wooden swivel chair in her father's study, she was heartily tired of cell phones. And with the way the evening had turned out.

She'd thought it had started out well enough, especially when Ethan had made the invitation to have dinner with him. His remark about not showing weakness or vulnerability was interesting, giving her a glimpse into how he operated, and how she should operate to get what she needed. But then James had arrived and the night had gone south in a hurry.

Business. She almost smiled at that. That blonde Morgan had passed on her walk to the main house hadn't been dressed for business, at least not the kind Morgan had thought Ethan meant. Tight designer jeans, boots with spike heels, a clinging black sweater and platinum-blond hair. With a fleeting look at her, the woman had dismissed Morgan out of hand and hurried right on past her to the guest house.

Morgan got up and went up to her bedroom, put away the clothes she'd dropped on the bed earlier, then undressed. By the time she stepped into the shower, she was practically laughing at the situation. The woman had been beautiful, a woman someone like Ethan Grace must attract like moths to a flame. Hell, even she was attracted to the man.

Her hand stilled from smoothing soap on her skin as it hit her how true that thought was. She started soaping her skin again and shut her eyes to the image of him she had in her mind. Was he naked? No. He hadn't been naked when she first met him. But attractive? "Damn straight," she muttered as she lifted her face to the heat of the stream of water.

She heard the phone ring and wished she could ignore it. But that was a luxury she didn't have. She got out, still soapy, and picked up the receiver of the phone her dad had installed outside the bathroom door. Practically a phone for every room and not one cordless one in the lot. They were "too undependable," her father would say.

"Dr. Morgan," she answered.

"Doc, it's Willie Short. I've got trouble here."

Willie was a bartender at the Ship's Rail bar in town. From the commotion in the background, he was at work. "What kind of trouble?"

"Some guy started a fight and split Jimmy James's head open. Jimmy's saying he's okay, but he don't look it to me. He's bleeding like a stuck pig."

Morgan wasn't sure what a stuck pig would bleed like, but she got the idea. She glanced at the clock by the phone. "Get a clean towel, put it on the wound and I'll be there soon."

She hung up, stepped back in the shower to rinse off the soap, then dried and dressed quickly. She was at the bar in ten minutes flat, and when she checked Jimmy James, a wiry little guy with a narrow face and scraggly mustache, she understood what Willie meant. Jimmy was bleeding all over the place. It was an easy fix and taking him to the clinic wouldn't be necessary. It took her half an hour and six stitches to put Jimmy back together again, and by the time she put on the last strip of bandage, Jimmy James was stone-cold sober and muttering about how the other guy sneaked up on him.

Willie, a stocky middle-aged man with more hair in his full beard than on the top of his head, was drying glasses at the bar as Morgan sat on one of the bar stools. She'd been in here a handful of times in her life and had to admit that it had real "atmosphere." At least, if you called everything pirate-and-pub-themed atmosphere. Lots of rough wood, leaded glass, smokey mirrors, stone walls and a sign over the door that read, Now You Know Why Roger Was So Jolly.

"Can I offer you a drink, Doc?" Willie asked, coming to where she sat.

She hadn't touched the wine at Ethan's so she agreed to a small brandy. She took a sip as soon as Willie brought it and felt the comforting heat slip down her throat. "Thanks for that."

"Thank you for coming over."

"Two blocks isn't that far to come," she said as she put down her snifter and looked around at the handful of people sitting at the scattering of rough tables and small booths. She was the only one at the bar. "Pretty quiet, except for the fight, huh?"

"Since the festival, I don't mind quiet nights." He started rubbing the bar top with his rag. "I'm more curious what the trouble was up at the Grace estate tonight."

That got her attention. "What?"

"My Sylvia's working up there on that party they're throwing for Joe Lawrence."

"She said there was trouble?"

"Said she saw you up there earlier tonight, and when she was leaving, they called for that private helicopter to come on over, that they needed to get someone to the mainland real quick. Sylvia said it sounded like an emergency and thought it was maybe something medical, since you were there and all."

Morgan couldn't explain the way her heart started beating faster, or why there was a surge of light-headedness at the thought that something had happened to Ethan. Had he taken pills before she'd arrived then drank wine with that woman? Or maybe he'd taken another fall? "When did it happen?"

"Two hours ago, maybe. Sylvia came by on her way home and told me. I'd heard that copter fly over myself." He frowned at her. "Was it a medical thing with you there and all?"

"Not that I know of." She fingered her snifter, then took her cell phone out of her jacket pocket. Even as she flipped it open, she realized she didn't have a number for Ethan's main house, much less for the guest house. She should have let it go—if they needed a doctor, they knew where she was. But she couldn't. "Willie, do you have any idea what the number is up there at the estate?"

Chapter Six

With luck, Willie happened to have the number—courtesy of Sylvia—and Morgan was already punching in the number. There was no formal greeting as she expected there to be. "Hello?" The voice was familiar.

"Hi, this is Dr. Morgan Kelly."

"What can I do for you?" It was James.

"Someone said you had a medical emergency up there right after I left, and I thought I'd check to see if I could be of any help."

"No, there's no medical emergency. I don't know what they were talking about."

"I heard the helicopter was called in."

He laughed, a short bark of a sound. "Oh, that was for a friend of the boss's who had to get back right away. The ferry was shut down for the night so we had to get Scooter to give us a hand."

"Mr. Grace is okay?"

"He's just fine."

The light-headedness came back in a rush from the ridiculous amount of relief that surged through her. "Oh, good."

"Do you want me to put you through to the boss?"

She hesitated, then rejected the idea of talking to Ethan. "No, I was just checking. Sorry to bother you."

"No bother. Small towns sure do have their own grapevine, don't they?"

"Yes, they do. Thanks," she replied and hit the end button. "It's nothing," she said, knowing Willie was all ears as he cleaned a glass. "Just getting a guest to the mainland."

"Those rich guys. Must be nice," he muttered and headed down the bar to serve a man who had just taken a seat.

Morgan stared at the remainder of her brandy, then downed it in one gulp. So much for sipping. She told herself her reaction to the possibility that Ethan had had a medical emergency was that if he'd needed to go to the mainland for treatment, there wouldn't be enough time for her to talk to him about her father's predicament. She refused to think about the other reason why she overreacted as she did.

She almost motioned to Willie to refill her glass, then stopped. No more brandy for her; she was ready to leave. Picking up the black bag she'd brought with her that her father had used for years for house calls, she spotted Jimmy James playing darts at the back of the bar. "Jimmy James?" she called.

The tiny man turned. "Yeah, Doc?"

"My office, tomorrow?"

"You got it, and thanks," he said before he went back to his game.

She left, stepping out into the bone-chilling cold of the night streets. For once the sky was almost clear, the stars twinkling in the moonless darkness. She tucked her chin into her collar and headed down the sidewalk for home. An hour later she sat at the old wooden table in the small yellow-and-white kitchen sorting through the box labeled House Matters that she'd found in her father's study.

It hadn't taken her long to find the original lease he'd signed for the medical office building. She read through it, and found, to her surprise, that it had been an open lease with no termination date. Leasing buildings for the clinic she worked at in Seattle had taught her one thing—get everything in writing since the city raised rents almost monthly. But her father's rent started at a minuscule amount, with the proviso, "to be adjusted as deemed fit." She knew his monthly payment was now ten times the original sum.

Her mother had dealt with the finances when she'd been alive, and Morgan didn't understand how she'd let him do this. Then again, her father did pretty much what he wanted. Only one sheet of paper outlined rules regarding the building where they had their offices, stating, "renovation of abandoned structures on the land is done at the expense of the lessor, and fees are nonrefundable upon termination of lease." Her father trusted everyone and probably thought this would never happen.

She sat back with a heavy sigh. No compensation? What was her dad thinking when he signed the papers?

She was startled when the phone on the wall rang. "Dr. Kelly."

"Hello there, Dr. Kelly. It's Ethan Grace."

She didn't have to be told the name of the man on the other end. She'd known immediately who it was as soon as he spoke. She closed her eyes, and wondered if she was getting sick. Her head felt dizzy again, the way it had in the bar. It couldn't have anything to do with this man, not both times. "Hello, Mr. Grace."

"Ethan," he told her.

"What do you need?"

"James told me you'd called earlier."

"Oh," she said as she sat back in the chair. "Someone told me a helicopter was rushed to your house, and I thought that, since you've been sick, there might have been a medical emergency, maybe another fall or something."

"None of the above."

He didn't explain any more, and she didn't ask. "Sorry I bothered Mr. Evans."

There was a pause, and Morgan wondered for a minute if their call had been disconnected.

"Morgan, I'm sorry we got interrupted this evening. I was looking forward to dinner."

She didn't know why his words took her off guard. She was sorry they were interrupted, too, and knew that, once again, he'd given her an opening she shouldn't waste. "We'll do it again."

"My thoughts exactly," he said softly, and she felt her breath catch in her chest. "How about tomorrow evening?"

Then she had an idea. Each time she'd spoken to Ethan, he'd been at his own place, in his comfort zone, and she certainly wasn't anywhere near her comfort zone when visiting the estate. "Do you get out at all?" she asked.

"I'm not a prisoner," he said. "Why?"

"I was thinking that with it being the middle of the week, things should be pretty quiet around here, but I still can't afford to be gone too much. So, if you could manage it, how would you like to come here, to my house, for dinner?"

There was silence, then, "The doctor cooks, too?"

"I told you when we had the discussion about grog that the doctor doesn't cook. But I order in, and quite effectively I might add. I could pick you up, if you need me to."

"I can get there."

"How about seven? You know where I live, don't you?"

"Everyone on the island does. And I've been there a few times when I was a kid."

"Really?" She didn't remember any Grace being a patient of her father's.

"Yeah, I got carried away when my friends were playing pirate and I lost the battle. I had to walk the plank, which had been balanced on a rock near the water. Whatever weight Joe or Evan used to balance it weighed a whole lot less than I did. I got on it, hit the point of no return and the whole damn thing shot up behind me, then came down on top of my head. Head wounds really bleed. Mine sure did."

"I never knew you had been a patient of Dad's."

She heard him chuckle. "I wouldn't expect you to know. I remember your mother being there and being very kind. She'd been holding a tiny baby, who cried the entire time I was there."

"Oh," she said, and since she was an only child, there was no question who the baby had been. She just didn't know why it should feel so odd thinking of Ethan seeing her as a baby and a crying one at that. "You were okay?"

"Your dad gave me eight stitches just above my hairline, and told me that I was a shame to my lineage." He laughed softly and she closed her eyes as the sound seemed to seep into her. "He said not to lose again, but if I messed up and had to walk the plank, I should make sure Joe and Evan stood on the other end to keep the board in place."

"And did you walk the plank again?" she asked as she opened her eyes to the emptiness around her.

"No, I didn't. I didn't want to shame Bartholomew Grace."

The humor in his voice only made the house seem more barren to her, and she was aware of a tingling in her right hand—she was holding the receiver so tightly that it almost hurt, and she eased her grip. Thankfully the line beeped right then. "Sorry, there's a call waiting. I need to—"

"Of course. Sickness waits for no man," he said. "See you tomorrow night at seven."

The silence in her ear lasted for only a second as she answered the other call. "Dr. Morgan," she said.

"Dr. Morgan here, too."

"Oh, Dad, hi," she said, surprised to hear her father's voice on the other end.

"You sound tired. I didn't wake you, did I?"

"No, I'm not sleeping. I was on the other line, and—"

"Got an emergency?" he asked quickly.

Not medical, she thought. "No, just talking."

"With whom?"

She almost told him, then thought better of it. There was no sense in bringing Ethan's name into this right now. "No one important," she said. "So, how's your vacation going?"

"It is wonderful being in the sun and relaxing."

He sounded more weary than excited. "But?"

"But nothing. I'm enjoying myself." There was a soft voice speaking indiscernible words in the background. "I've been meeting new people, who aren't patients," he said with a chuckle. "I'm expanding my horizons and thinking about a lot of things."

"Like what?"

"Life, our life. I am getting older and life is getting shorter."

"Oh, Dad, you're not that old."

"Not yet, but I'm getting there. When I get back, we'll sit down and have a talk. There are some things you need to know."

She felt a tightness in her chest at his tone. Was it defeat, tiredness or sadness? She wasn't sure, but it wasn't like her dad to talk like this. "What's going on?" she asked. "Are you all right?" She swallowed hard, remembering how pale he'd been before he left. "Are you sick?"

"No, Morgan, I'm not sick. You sound just like your mom, always thinking the worst. All I meant was I can't do what I used to, and my patients deserve my best. I'm afraid I can't give it to them anymore."

She closed her eyes tightly. "Just like that, you think you're over the hill?"

"No, not just like that. You've been gone a lot, and things have changed, so…" His voice trailed off. "The timing isn't very good, but maybe this is for the best. You can think about it before I get back."

"Think about what?" she asked, but was already somewhat certain about what was coming.

"Taking over for me. Helping me make the urgent-care clinic a reality, so I can retire without regrets. Maybe I can work part-time for a while or act as a consultant. But just think about taking over my practice soon. I'd be proud if you did—you're a wonderful physician."

Morgan felt a weight falling around her shoulders and she couldn't do a thing to shake it off. Why now? Why when the future of the clinic was such a mess? "Dad, we'll talk when you get back, but there's something I need to tell you about, about the house and office."

"I'm sorry," he said. "This connection comes and goes, and you're breaking up. Damn wireless phones. They aren't worth their weight in pennies. What did you say?"

She bit her lip hard. This wasn't the time to bring up the lease. "Nothing. We'll talk later."

"Yes, we will," he said. "I love you."

"I love you, too," she said softly, then hung up.

She buried her head in her hands. She loved the work she did in Seattle, helping the people in the poorer sections of the city. Although the money was almost nonexistent, that hadn't been her motivation for taking the job, any more than money had been her father's motivation for being the doctor on the island. The work they did fed them in some way she hadn't even known existed until she started practicing medicine herself.

She stood, sighing deeply as she headed into her father's study. She had records to go over, but that didn't stop her from thinking about what her father had said, and how very much she hoped she could talk Ethan in to accepting her offer or, at least, get him to give her more time to arrange an alternative.

The phone on the desk rang again, and she stared at it for a long moment before reaching for it. "Dr. Kelly." It was her service this time, and she actually breathed a sigh of relief that it wasn't her father or Ethan.

BY THE TIME James drove Ethan to Morgan's house the next evening, they were fifteen minutes late and Ethan had a hell of a time getting out of the car. He hadn't thought about what he'd wear, and the black slacks he'd chosen had to be cut from the cuff to the knee to get the damn cast through. Once he had them on, he pulled on a black sweater, and then knew he had to put something on his feet. James had found an oversized sock to cover the foot of the cast and helped him find a simple loafer for his left foot.

Ethan felt like some fool teenager getting dressed, and James obviously thought he looked like one. As they went up the walkway to Morgan's father's house, James said, "Well Scrooge sure doesn't live here. I thought the office was decorated when we passed it, but take a look in there."

Ethan had noticed the multicolored lights in the office windows and a huge sign above the main door declaring Happy Holidays. Now as he looked up at the Kelly house instead of at his feet as he took each step on the rough walkway, he saw white twinkling lights lining the front windows that were decorated with holly wreaths, and pine boughs on the jambs. There were no lights outside, but a four-foot-tall statue of Santa stood sentry by the door. "Bah humbug," he joked.

"I told you, you should have worn your elf outfit. But no, you had to put on regular clothes," James mocked as he followed behind him.

Ethan got to the porch and barely knocked. Morgan opened the heavy wood door. When she smiled up at him, all the pain and hassle to make it here had been worth it for him to see her again. "Hi, there. Sorry we're late."

She stood back, and he skimmed his gaze over her simple golden silk blouse, pleated brown slacks and low heels. Her hair was loose around her shoulders, and there was just a touch of color on her lips. "No problem. I just got the tree to stand up on its own, so your timing worked out fine," she said and motioned them inside.

He hobbled past her and right into a large living room filled with Christmas decorations. A bare six-foot-tall tree was by a stone fireplace, but the rest of the room certainly wasn't naked. Boxes of ornaments were stacked on the floor, and pine boughs laced with lights draped the large mantel above a roaring fire. Garlands swagged around the top of the walls and more twinkle lights outlined every entrance to the room. He glanced to the right through a well-lit arch into the dining room. More pine boughs and lights, and the large table was set for two, with a red-and-green-plaid tablecloth and matching napkins.

He stopped next to a large couch and turned to face the fireplace. "Everything set here?" James asked.

"Sure. I'll call when I'm ready to come home."

Morgan shook her head, making her hair drift around her shoulders. Ethan liked the way the curls picked up the glow from the flickering lights. "No, no, I can take you back to your place. He doesn't have to make the trip again."

"Are you sure?" James asked. "I get paid to lug him around."

"I'm very sure," Morgan said and motioned Ethan to the couch. "Please, sit down. You shouldn't be on your feet so much."

"That's what I've been telling him, but I'm no doctor."

Ethan ignored James, putting the crutch against the back of the sofa, then he made his way around to sink into the cushions. Two ottomans were set between the couch and the hearth, pushed together to make a makeshift coffee table. Before he knew what was happening, Morgan lifted his cast to prop his leg on the closest ottoman. "My dad uses these all the time to relax, and they're just about the right height for you." She straightened. "Better?"

"Much."

"Good. Keep it elevated as much as you can."

"As I said, I was telling him the same thing, but since I'm not a doctor, he doesn't listen to me."

Ethan didn't even look at James. "Your idea of medical advice is only to let people with blue felt-tipped pens sign the cast."

"That's right," James said. "Stick with the blues."

Ethan didn't take his eyes off Morgan, who was watching James. "Would you like to stay for dinner? I ordered more than enough."

Before Ethan could jump in and tell her that James wasn't about to stay, his friend did it for him. "Thanks, but I have things to see and people to do. Or the other way around."

Morgan smiled at that. "I get the idea."

"Then I'm out of here. Merry Christmas." Ethan soon heard the door close behind him.

"Nice guy," Morgan said as she glanced at Ethan. "Can you drink?"

"I can manage," he said.

"I meant, your medication—?"

"None recently."

"Okay, what would you like? Beer, wine, eggnog?"

"Anything but eggnog."

"Allergic?"

"To the taste," he said and was rewarded with one of her quick smiles.

"Got it," she said and headed for the dining room. "I'll be right back."

Ethan sat forward, managed to get his jacket off, then tossed it next to him onto the couch. In a moment, Morgan was back with a two wineglasses and an opened bottle. She poured some wine for both of them and handed him his drink. "Do you mind if I just put some things on this tree? It looks pitiful."

"Not at all."

She crouched by the boxes, opening one after the other. Ethan had no trouble talking to anyone, but for some reason he had to fish around in his mind for something to say. It wasn't that he couldn't think of anything to chat about, but nothing that came immediately to mind was right. He certainly wasn't going to tell her that he liked the way her hips looked in her slacks or that he really enjoyed the way the fire brought out the rich color of her hair. Instead, he said, "This place hasn't changed much from what I remember, except for the Christmas explosion."

She chuckled softly as her blue eyes met his. "A Christmas explosion? Yeah, I guess it is, isn't it?" She stood and started hanging silver baubles on the branches of the fir tree. "I haven't done much decorating in the past few years. My mom used to do the house up completely, inside and out." She bent to get more balls. "I don't think my dad had the heart to do it much after she was gone, and Sharon, the nurse in my office, took over decorating duties, at least in the office."

"I noticed on the way here."

She chuckled, a soft, rich sound. "Sharon goes a bit overboard about Christmas." She kept working, her back to him, so he couldn't read her expression. "I noticed you don't have any Christmas decorations at the guest house. Is that because you don't like the holidays or is it just that you don't have enough time for them?"

"There's never enough time," he said and drank some wine.

She crouched again and pushed her hand behind the tree. The next instant lights flashed to life on it, all green and twinkling. He hadn't noticed them when he'd arrived. "What do you usually do for Christmas then?"

He thought he should offer to help, but he liked just watching her. "I send expensive presents and stay out of the way."

She turned to him, a package of old-fashioned tinsel in her hands. Her nose scrunched up. "That sounds like 'bah humbug' to me."

With James he'd had fun acting Scrooge-like, but with her, he felt as if she were reprimanding him. It didn't help that he immediately had the urge to defend his choices about the holidays. "When I was a kid, the house was always decorated. Okay, it was done by a service, but we had a tree, usually around ten feet tall, all trimmed in a single color. A blue Christmas one year, a red Christmas the next, a gold Christmas after that. You get the idea. Then we had a formal sit-down meal, usually squab and snow peas."

"No turkey and cranberries?"

"I don't remember having them."

She grimaced, almost as if she pitied him for not having garish decorations and a huge turkey in the middle of a table set with dishes decorated with holly and done in reds and greens. She turned back to the tree and started to toss tinsel methodically onto the boughs. No fancy garlands or twisted foil, just long strands of silver that clung to the branches. "I can't imagine that."

He finished his wine. "I didn't feel deprived," he said matter-of-factly.

"I didn't mean that," she said quickly, and he wished he'd kept that to himself. "That never crossed my mind." She stood back as if studying her handiwork.

That brought a rough chuckle from him. "Now there's a

visual—a Grace deprived." He was shocked at the tinge of bitterness he heard in his voice. It made no sense, but he actually found himself wondering what it would have been like to have had a Christmas with a real tree, homemade decorations and enough turkey to feed an army.

"Squabs and snow peas are definitely not the sign of deprivation," she teased, and came to take a seat on the chair to his left.

She brought her wineglass with her, cradling it, but not drinking. Why did he suddenly feel as if he'd missed something basic all those years? No, it wasn't something. It was *someone*. A person who seemed thrilled by all of this, who probably looked forward to gorging on turkey and to making the paper chains and popping the popcorn for the clove-studded oranges that hung in each doorway. He studied her silhouette as she admired the tree, and knew that he'd just described Morgan Kelly. "You love turkey, don't you?"

That brought her attention back to him as she said, almost wistfully, "And cranberries and pumpkin pie and squash soup. My mom used to make the best squash soup."

He wasn't going to admit that he hated pumpkin pie and had never had good squash soup. "Very traditional," he said just to fill the space, but knew it was the wrong thing to say when she frowned.

"Tradition isn't a bad thing. It's what binds today with the past." She looked around the room. "And it's good to have a place that you know is always going to be there, a place you can come back to and know that it's home. That it always will be home."

Now she looked almost pained. This wasn't what he'd imagined on the way here. He'd wanted small talk, to find out more about her and to figure out how she managed to get under his skin. Now all he wanted to do was erase whatever had caused her discomfort. At least he thought that's what he wanted until she spoke again.

"That's why it's so important not to lose all of this." She met his gaze directly. "Do you understand that?"

He thought for a moment that she'd launch into the clinic's problems and the lease termination, but she didn't. Surprisingly, she waved any further discussion off with a flick of her hand. "I am not going to get all maudlin about this." She glanced at his cast. "How is your leg?"

"Fine, thanks."

"Well, thank God you were in a place where you could get good medical help when the accident happened."

He'd been wrong. He knew exactly where this was going, and he would have gotten up and walked out, if he could have done it with any sense of dignity. "I was at the hospital in two minutes," he admitted, trying not to clench his jaw.

She looked away but didn't let it go. "That's great. You're lucky it didn't happen over here."

He was determined to not let this get out of hand. "Then I would have had a pretty doctor who would have come to my rescue." He met her gaze when she turned to him and finished with, "And you're a better alternative than an EMT, believe me."

She opened her mouth to say something, but stopped when the phone rang. She moved quickly, reaching for a phone on a table by her chair.

"Dr. Morgan." She listened, asked a few questions about a fever and skin color, then said, "I'll be right there. Keep cool cloths on his forehead and under his arms. Cool, not cold."

She hung up, set her drink by the phone, then turned to Ethan as she got to her feet. "That was Alegra Reynolds. Joe's boy's sick. I have to go."

He didn't think twice as she hurried out of the room.

Putting his glass down by the open bottle of wine, he grabbed his jacket and quickly put it on. "I'm going with you."

"You don't have to," she said, and he turned to reach for his crutch. She took out a well-worn, stereotypical doctor's black bag and set it on the floor, then retrieved her leather jacket from the closet. "Stay here and make yourself comfortable," she said.

He hobbled over to where she stood. "Are they at Joe's parents' place?" he asked, ignoring her suggestion.

"Yes, they are."

"Then let's go," he said and reached to open the door. She looked up at him then down at his cast before hurrying past him.

"I'll get the car," she called to him as she jogged out of sight.

He'd managed to close the door, which locked behind him, and get down the steps by the time he heard the car engine and saw headlights coming down the driveway around the side of the house. He met her at the end of the walk, and the passenger door to the old compact swung open for him.

"What's wrong with Alex?" he asked as she turned onto the main street and headed north.

"Alex? Oh, he's got a fever, blotches on his face and chest, and he's wheezing." She cast him a fleeting glance before looking ahead again.

"What do you think he might have?"

"He's a kid, and kids get anything that passes by them. Hopefully it's something simple."

He didn't want to ask, but he had to. "And if it's not?"

Her expression was tight with worry. "I don't know," she said, her voice barely above a whisper.

He kept his hand pressed to his thigh and didn't do what he wanted to do—touch her, tell her it would be okay. He wanted nothing more than to make everything okay. But that was impossible, and he'd never felt more helpless in his life.

Chapter Seven

They arrived at the sprawling bungalow north of the town in record time, and Morgan grabbed her medical bag as she opened the car door with her other hand. She hurried around the car at the same time the front door to the house opened and a woman appeared. "Dr. Kelly?" she called out.

"Yes, I'm here," Morgan responded, unable to get a good look at the woman because the light behind her made her little more than a tall, slender silhouette in the night. Morgan took the porch steps in one long stride. "Where is he?"

Morgan saw a strikingly pretty woman with pale blond hair caught in a ponytail, Alegra Reynolds was dressed in narrow-legged jeans along with a bulky blue sweater. At any other time she would have been a knockout; right now she looked scared to death. "The back bedroom, straight ahead."

Morgan went past her and stepped into a room of multiple shades of blue and decorated to cater to a little boy who obviously loved boats. Dropping her bag on the floor, she crouched next to the old-fashioned spool bed to get on eye level with Joe Lawrence's son. Fine straw-colored hair clung to his damp, flushed face, and his blue eyes seemed dull from sickness.

She reached to touch him and felt some relief to find that his fever wasn't too high. If it had been earlier, it had already broken. "I need to check you out, Alex, but I'll be quick," she promised and opened her bag. He lay still as she listened to his heart and lungs, took his temperature and felt for swollen glands at his throat. Her frantic heartbeat started to ease. Alex Lawrence was sick, but it looked as though a common cold, possibly the flu, but nothing that she couldn't handle.

She dropped her stethoscope into her bag, then breathed a soft sigh. "You're going to be fine," she promised softly. "You're going to be just fine. Just do everything Alegra and your daddy tell you to do, and you'll be better in a couple of days."

Alex's heavy-lidded eyes shifted to Alegra. "'Legga?" he whispered.

"I'm here," she said.

Alegra moved to take Morgan's place, dropping to her knees and taking the boy's hand in hers. With the other hand, she brushed his damp hair gently. "What's wrong with him?" she asked Morgan without looking at her.

"He's got a cold with minor lung involvement. He needs to stay in bed a few days, drink lots of juice. Give him soup and Popsicles—liquids of any sort." She took out a sample of cough syrup and set it on the nightstand. "I'll leave this for you so you don't need to go out tonight. Follow the directions. Tomorrow call the office and set up a follow-up visit just so I can make sure everything's under control."

"You're sure that it's not bad?" Alegra asked with obvious nervousness as she brushed the boy's cheek with her fingertips.

"Absolutely," Morgan said, then touched Alegra's shoulder. She could feel the tremors in the woman's body and knew she'd been terrified when she'd made the call. "You can relax. Believe me, kids get sick all the time, and you need to take care of yourself so you can be there for him."

Alegra laughed—a tight, nervous sound and finally glanced up at Morgan. "I wish I could." She really was lovely, but didn't exactly look like a woman who ran a successful line of exclusive boutiques called Alegra's Closets. "But it came out of nowhere. He was fine at dinner, and when they all left, I thought…I promised to take care of him, and I thought…" She bit her bottom lip, then spoke in a rush. "Thank you so much for coming, Dr. Kelly. I never thought anyone did house calls anymore."

"We're a small town around here, and house calls are the norm at this time of night. I'm glad to do it," Morgan said as she closed her bag. "And please, call me Morgan. When someone says Dr. Kelly, I look around for my father."

"I'm Alegra Reynolds. I'm Joe's fiancée."

"I've heard about you," Morgan said. "As I said, the island is just one small town when it comes to news about the residents."

Alegra grimaced. "I can imagine what they're saying about Joe's and my wedding preparations."

There had been some jokes because of Alegra's work, but most had just been happy for Joe that he'd found someone again. His first marriage had been a disaster and his son was the only good that had come out of it. "They're happy for both of you," she said truthfully.

Alegra turned back to Alex, who had quietly fallen asleep. "And we're happy," she said softly.

"Alegra?"

The voice coming from the doorway jarred Morgan and she was surprised to see Ethan standing there watching them. Alegra looked, too, then stood and crossed to him. "Ethan," she said, giving him a hug.

He smiled. "Things are okay with Alex?"

"They are now."

"Great."

"You know, we've barely had a chance to talk, and I've been wanting to thank you for all you're doing for us. We gave you such short notice, and we really were just going to have a small ceremony and a family party. But now it's a full-blown event, a big holiday thing."

He let her go as he shifted to readjust the crutch under his arm. "It's very full-blown," he said, his smile wry. "But you both deserve it and I'm glad to do it." He glanced past her at the sick child. "He deserves it, too."

"He's wonderful," Alegra said, then turned to Morgan, a quizzical expression on her face. "You two came together?"

"I tagged along," Ethan answered. "I heard it was Joe's boy and I came with the doctor."

"He's going to be okay," Morgan said as she picked up her bag and took one last look at the boy.

Alegra exhaled. "The first time Joe trusts me to watch him and look what happens."

Morgan crossed to her, putting her hand on Alegra's arm. "You did just fine. And kids get sick so suddenly, you don't have any warning. You did the right thing by calling me."

"I tried to call Joe's cell phone, but it rang in the kitchen." She smiled slightly. "He never remembers to take it with him. And I couldn't remember the name of the place they had gone to." She covered Morgan's hand with her own. "I don't know what I would have done without you."

"Alegra!"

A man's voice called through the house, right before a door slammed shut. Morgan hadn't seen Joe Lawrence since he was a teenager, but she recognized him right away—he was just a more mature version of the kid she'd seen so many years ago.

Alegra stayed where she was, twisting her hands together. "Joe, I'm sorry," she breathed. "It's Alex, he's sick and you didn't have your cell phone, and I called the doctor—"

Joe rushed to the bed and hunkered down by his son, who

was deep in sleep now. He reached to touch his small hand laying on the blue blanket. Alegra went toward the bed, but stopped short of where Joe was, her hands clasped so tightly her knuckles were white. "He's going to be okay," Alegra said quickly. "It's a cold. Morgan said he'll be fine."

Joe slowly stood and reached for Alegra. He hugged her close for a long moment, his face buried in her hair, his eyes closed. "You did just fine. Perfect," he whispered to her.

Morgan looked away, a bit uncomfortable to see the real connection these two people had. She literally jumped when Ethan put his hand on her shoulder. "Let's go," he mouthed.

Quietly they left the room, but they didn't get to the front door before Joe came running after them. "Hey there, you two," he called. "Thank you so much, Dr. Kelly. I'd heard you were back in town, but I didn't realize you were involved in your dad's practice."

"I'm taking over for Dad while he's on vacation."

Joe shook his head. "I don't believe that I've ever heard of Doc Kelly taking a vacation."

"That's why he's taking one now," she said.

His eyes, as blue as his son's, turned to Ethan. "What in the world are you doing here?"

"I'm with her," he said, motioning to Morgan with a nod.

Joe studied him, then grinned. "I know we didn't see each other much over the past four years, but you never told me you'd gone into medicine."

"No medical ambitions for me, but I was at Morgan's when she got the call. When I found out she was coming here, I hitched a ride to see what was going on."

"Thanks for showing up," he said soberly. "Thanks."

"He's your son," Ethan said in a low voice. "I'm just happy that he's going to be okay."

"As I said, thanks."

Even though Joe and Ethan hadn't seen each other for years, it was obvious to Morgan that they were close. It would have been easy for her to tell Ethan to stay and spend some time with Joe, but that would mean she'd give up her opening to talk to him about the land and the offices. She bit her lip, and the better part of her took over. "If you want to stay and—?"

"No, that's okay. I think we need to get going." He looked at Joe. "Drop by if you don't mind being run over by the hordes doing the prep work for your reception."

Joe grimaced. "Yeah, sorry about that. Roz is Alegra's right-hand person. When she got here, she took over and that was that. We just have to step aside and let her go."

"If you come over, go straight to the guest house—that's where you'll find me."

"Okay, great," Joe said.

Ethan glanced at Morgan. "Let's go."

She nodded to Joe, then turned and grabbed the door. The rain hadn't started, but fog was rolling in, and what moonlight showed came through the clouds in thin ribbons here and there. She heard Ethan shuffling behind her, the thump of his crutch striking the porch floor, then on the steps. She got into the car, and started the motor while he settled and shoved his crutch into the backseat.

"That turned out pretty well," he said with a sigh.

"We were very lucky," was all she said as they headed south on the deserted highway.

"It wasn't luck," Ethan replied. "You're a good doctor."

She held tightly to the steering wheel and took a breath as if she was bracing herself. She probably was since she wasn't sure just how Ethan would react to what she was going to say next. "No, it was luck."

"How do you figure that?"

"I was available, and the problem was simple."

Ethan shifted, and he must have hit his cast because she heard a thud, then he muttered, "Damn it," before he spoke again. "Then everything worked out."

She bit her lip. "This time."

"Do I need to ask what that means?" he asked, and she heard the hesitation in his voice.

She had his attention, but was uneasy about how to proceed. "I just meant my dad built a good practice on the island, and he's the best at basic medicine. Actually, he could have had a great career in diagnostic medicine. He can figure out symptoms better than any other doctor I've been around." She slowed as the lights from the town came closer. "He's really great."

"And so are you, obviously. It runs in the family."

She waved aside his compliment. "What I'm trying to say is that even Dad has his limitations. He's gifted but he still needs the tools to do what he needs to do. The clinic I work at in Seattle is nonprofit, but we have everything we need in an emergency, and one of the best hospitals in the city is right down the block." Now that she was talking, she couldn't stop. "We had a case just before I arrived home, an elderly man who came in with a pain in his leg. Didn't sound serious, but we checked him out and found a blood clot in the main artery in his thigh. I don't want to get too technical, but there's a procedure that, if it's done immediately, is almost always effective.

"It really is a simple procedure, but my father doesn't have the equipment to perform it if it happened here. If that person had to be taken to the mainland—even if he'd been flown by helicopter—the chances aren't good he'd survive. And if Alex had been in a position where he needed more than I could do for him…" She couldn't suppress a shiver. "I'm sorry. It's just hard sometimes, fearing you won't be able to help someone, and knowing there will come a time when you simply can't."

The glow of Christmas lights in town was blurred by the incoming fog, and she slowed as she got closer to her house. Ethan was silent, then as she signaled for the turn, he spoke. "I understand."

She stopped the car without making the turn and stared at him. "You do?" she asked, shocked that her rambling had translated into something that had made her point.

"No, not really. How could I? I don't deal with life and death in my business, but I can appreciate the pressure you're under."

She turned abruptly into the parking area of the offices, then drove past to the house behind. How could he understand? Everything in his life was black-and-white; in hers there were so many shades of gray. Instead of parking the car in the garage, she stopped by the porch steps. Undoing her seat belt, she faced Ethan. "I don't deal in life and death all the time. A cold isn't life and death. A broken leg isn't life and death. But if there are complications with a problem, even a small one—" she shrugged "—sometimes there are no second chances."

He startled her by touching her hand where she'd pressed it to the console. She tensed but didn't pull back. "Second chances come along, but you can't count on them. So my philosophy has always been to live life the way you want. I don't stress over what could be, but deal with whatever happens here and now."

ETHAN HAD WATCHED Morgan with Alex, and he'd seen the passion she had for her work. He wouldn't even think about her bedside manner. He could remember how she'd been with him when she'd found him after the fall—and he'd wanted to touch her ever since. No, he wanted a lot more then just a touch. Now he could feel the silky heat of her skin under his fingers. Would he ever see her look like this again? Would her lips be parted seductively? Would they be completely alone?

Before he could do more than seriously think of making the most of the present, a horn sounded behind the car. Morgan jumped and he twisted around to see someone right behind them, the car's headlights almost blinding him despite the fast-falling fog.

"Dr. Kelly!" A kid maybe sixteen years old, wearing a bulky down jacket and a Santa hat with a bell, knocked on Morgan's window. "I thought that was you going by," he said after Morgan opened her door. "Ed said to bring the food on over." He held up two large white bags. "When I got here and you were nowhere around, I figured you had some emergency or something, so we kept it warm for you."

"I totally forgot," Morgan said and reached for her black bag before closing the door. "Come on with me and I'll get your money."

The two of them took off to the house as if Ethan didn't exist. He quickly grabbed his crutch and hobbled after them. By the time he got up the steps and across the porch to go through the open front door, Morgan was handing the boy some bills. "Tell Ed I really appreciate him doing this."

"Great tip," the kid said when he looked down at the money in his hand. Then he touched his Santa hat in salute and turned to leave. "Merry Christmas," he said, then stopped when he saw Ethan in the doorway. "Enjoy."

Ethan swung the door shut, then looked over at Morgan, who was taking off her jacket. "I forgot all about the food delivery," she said as she laid the coat on the couch back, then picked up the two bags she'd placed on the floor. "It's nice that Ed took care of things."

"Nice," he agreed.

She held up the bags. "Let's eat, then. It's hot."

She led the way into the dining room, and Ethan followed her, taking the chair she indicated.

"I didn't know what you'd prefer, so I kept it simple," she said as she opened the containers.

He looked down at the food. Simple was right—two steaks, baked potatoes, mixed vegetables, a green salad and crusty rolls. "I don't mind simple," he said.

"Good thing." She went back into the living room and brought in their glasses and the wine bottle they left open. Setting them on the table within Ethan's reach, she sat to his left.

"I hope the steaks aren't like leather," she said.

"Wine helps everything," he said and reached for the bottle to pour himself a drink. He looked at Morgan and held up the bottle.

"No, I don't think so," she said.

"Is one drink your limit?"

She shook her head and reached to take a steak from the container before pushing the food closer to him. "I just shouldn't drink much, not when I can have an emergency at any minute and the fog is coming in."

"I'm not driving," he said, drank some wine, then reached for his steak.

They ate in silence for a while, then he laid down his fork. Morgan glanced at him, then his food. "Not hungry?"

"I'm fine," he said and took another sip of wine.

She reached for a roll and tore it into two pieces. "I owe you an apology," she said before putting the bread on her plate without tasting it.

He couldn't think of why she'd be apologizing to him, but was intrigued. "How so?"

She sat back and met his gaze. "I talk too much. After a crisis, I have this tendency to talk and talk and talk about what happened, and what could have or might have or should have happened."

"Second-guessing yourself?"

She shook her head. "No, not that. I learned in med school that a doctor who second-guesses himself or herself is no good to anyone. Any hesitation could be deadly."

He understood that. "Business is like that, too. You can't indulge in 'what-ifs' or 'should haves,' or you're dead in the water." He realized what he'd said and gave her a self-deprecating grin. "Sorry, bad choice of words."

She smiled, but it was tight and didn't touch her eyes. "Well, you can imagine how much that's magnified for a doctor." She shook her head. "I don't know how my dad does it here. He's the only doctor, doing it on hope and a prayer, and he still keeps going. At least he was…or he is…"

Over the years Ethan had learned to read people and Morgan had a face that registered emotions as clearly as anyone he'd ever known. When she'd been with Alex, she'd been genuinely worried and concern. Now he thought there was sadness lingering in her eyes, and her voice held a tinge of it. "Is something wrong with your father?"

"Wrong?" she echoed, then shook her head. "No, it's just, he's on this vacation—the first one in years—and now he's suddenly talking about retiring."

"And that's a bad thing?"

She looked down at the table. "No, of course not. It's just something I hadn't really considered him doing right now."

"You expected him to work forever?"

Sitting back, she tucked her hair behind her ears, making herself look remarkably young and very vulnerable. He could see a light dusting of freckles across her nose. "You never think of your parents getting old. When my mother died, there was no warning. She had an aneurysm and it…" She bit her lip. "But Dad, he's been around a long time, and been a doctor my whole life, right here, on this island, on this land."

"Are you taking over for him?" Ethan asked, figuring that was why she was so interested in the cost of the property here.

"I've always intended to, sooner or later. I love the island and the people. That's why I became a doctor, because of Dad. But he's the real Dr. Kelly, and if he's not here, if this place is gone, it just seems…"

He studied her as her voice died out, and that sadness seemed to grow in her. He thought of saying, "Life goes on," but trite words weren't needed then. "You are Dr. Kelly, and you'll take over and do as well as your dad, maybe even better."

She shook her head, and laid her napkin over her partially eaten food. "No, I couldn't be better. And now I'm not sure that I can do this. I can't say I'll help the islanders when I know that if they have an emergency, and need care I can't give them, their lives could be at risk. Could you live that way?"

God, he didn't like this. He didn't like to be on the receiving end of some sort of spot quiz when he obviously didn't have the right answers. "How would I know? I'm not a doctor."

"But I am. And I can tell you that the medical services on the island are puny at best. That's why a clinic with beds and up-to-date equipment is so badly needed." She rested her elbows on the table and leaned toward him. "Can you see why we need to be here, why we need to be able to build the clinic?"

Although he sympathized with Morgan and her dad, Ethan knew there was little he could do. She couldn't afford to buy the property anyway so there was no point in discussing the situation further. "I think it's time for me to go." He pushed to his feet and reached for the crutch. "I'll call James and he—"

"No," she said, getting up quickly. "I said I'd take you home and I will."

"What if there's an emergency?" he pointed out as she faced him.

"I'll figure out something if that happens," she said and turned to get her coat. He followed, got his own jacket off the couch and managed to get it on. "Ready?" she asked, car keys in her hand.

He looked down at her, at the blue eyes shadowed by incredibly long lashes, and at her even teeth worrying her bottom lip. "Morgan, I told you, this whole thing isn't up to me. Talk to—"

"I called the office as you suggested, and Jaye Fleming either wasn't there or he's avoiding me. Besides, I was told the property wasn't available. Period. Your company is going to take all of this and destroy it so they can build a yuppie haven with a view."

All of his working life Ethan saw that destruction meant building and renewal. The old building, old house and empty land they were standing on might someday hold a small clinic, but the value wasn't there. "Oh, Morgan, even if it was for sale, you couldn't afford it."

He knew the minute he said the words, she saw a glimmer of hope. "What if we could get the money together or get financing of some sort?"

He hated to do it, not when the thought brought a light to her eyes, but he stopped her in her tracks. "That's not going to happen."

"But, what if—?"

"Business isn't about 'what-ifs' or dreams." He adjusted the crutch under his armpit. He wanted to leave now. "Bottom line is, the land is more valuable developed than it is being used like this."

"And that's what counts, isn't it? How much money there is for your business and your investors in doing it?"

"I'm not in business for the love of it," he muttered, and he didn't love arguing with her, either.

She stared up at him, then released a heavy sigh. "I'm sorry. I talk too much. I get too passionate about things. I get carried away. I'm sorry."

He met her gaze and wondered what would happen if her passion were directed at him, instead of this land business? He let go of that thought with a shake of his head. "Let's go," he said and went to the door.

Chapter Eight

Morgan could have smacked herself for what she'd said. She hadn't meant to get into her family's problems right then with Ethan, and she knew she'd gone way too far when Ethan's expression had grown tight and he'd asked to leave. By the time she got behind the wheel, he was settled, his crutch in the back and his gaze directly ahead. "Lots of fog," she said for something to fill the void between them.

"Yeah," he replied, but didn't say anything else.

She gripped the steering wheel and backed out, then turned onto the main street going north. The fog was so heavy the streetlamps created halos of light in the veil around them. She watched the center line, keeping to the right and hoping that if there was a car ahead, she'd see its lights before she ran into it.

She felt the nerves at the base of her neck tightening, and found herself talking again, but this time, she said anything she could that didn't have to do with her problems. "I remember a fog like this when I was a kid and Boyd Posey, who works at the newspaper, had to drive home with his head out the window so he could see the road in front of him."

Ethan didn't respond other than a general, "Hmm."

"You never get used to this," she said. "Not any more than

you get used to the rain. I wonder why Bartholomew Grace thought this place was so wonderful."

He finally spoke up. "He didn't. He came here because it was the safest place for him. A place he could defend easily, and a place most other ships would go past because of the peninsula that blocks it from view from the open ocean. It made sense. I don't think he ever thought of it as home."

"Why did your family stay on the island after the house was ruined?"

"I don't know. Few of them stayed longer than they had to."

"You didn't, did you?"

"I went away to college and didn't come back until my parents took off for France and left the estate empty."

"But you don't live here?"

"I come off and on. And the house comes in handy for things like Joe's party."

The fog thinned a bit as they drove under a canopy of huge trees. "Where is your home when you're not here?"

He hesitated, then said, "Usually San Francisco. Sometimes in Seattle. A few times a year in New York. What about you?"

She almost said Seattle and the tiny apartment she had there near the docks, but she didn't. *This* was her home. The island. The house. The offices. A view that his company was going to charge millions for people to enjoy. No place had ever felt like this place to her. "Right here," she said.

She spotted the turn for his house and pulled into the driveway. The gates stood open, and she drove through. The fog hid almost everything, except the curve to the drive and the soft glow of the lights in the huge house as they approached it. "Over there," Ethan said, and motioned her to a side entrance under a stone archway.

She pulled to a stop and didn't look at the man next to her. She stared out into the night, waiting for him to say good-night and get out, but he didn't. "I thought we were going to start all over again," he said.

She'd told him truthfully about her shortcomings. Her father had always said her passionate nature was her blessing and her curse, that she was too much like him in some ways. She acted quickly, didn't think enough and fought for what she wanted. Maybe that was why she was constantly putting her relationship with Ethan at risk. There was something about him that frustrated her but wanted him at the same time. And she needed him. She knew he was the only one who could make this situation with her father all right, even if he said he couldn't.

She forced out the words she hoped would break down the wall that she had begun building between them, by what she'd said at the house, and hoped for the best. "We can start all over again…again," she said softly.

"Second chances," he murmured. "I think I'm starting to like that concept. Let's do it."

"Okay," she agreed. "I'll try to watch what I say, and try to be more diplomatic."

"That should be interesting," he said, and now she knew he was smiling.

"I have a temper. And I speak before I think and I say things…" She knew he wouldn't buy it that she'd just let the whole land business go, so she told him honestly, "The land and house and clinic are monumentally important to me, but I'll deal with it. You've made it very clear that there isn't anything you can do, and I understand that." She grew tense when Ethan kept quiet and found herself making a silly joke to try to lighten the moment. "Even yuppies deserve to have a view, I guess."

He didn't laugh, but countered with, "Can I be honest, too?"

Her stomach clenched at his words and she wished she hadn't eaten anything. "Of course."

He leaned toward her and his hand found hers where she had it pressed hard against her thigh. His fingers closed around hers, and she didn't fight the connection. It didn't occur to her to pull back until he'd turned her hand over in his and touched her exposed palm with the forefinger of his free hand. "Something I learned in the business world is to watch a person's eyes, but also what they do with their hands while you're negotiating with them."

She looked down at her hand in his and withdrew from his touch. "What are you talking about?" she asked, balling her hand into a fist on her lap.

"That," he said, nodding down at her clenched hand. Quickly, she pushed it between her hip and the console. "Relax," he said, and all that did was make her nervousness accelerate twofold. "I asked Jaye about development of the property."

That startled her. "Why didn't you say that to begin with?"

"I figured you didn't need more bad news."

Her heart sank. "What bad news?"

He proceeded to give her a monetary value that had been put on the joint parcels of land, and it stunned her. "And that's a conservative figure," he added.

Conservative? It was beyond anything she'd thought of, and way beyond any amount she could raise if she had the rest of her life to work and save and beg and borrow. "Oh," she breathed. "Oh."

"What you think you could do isn't going to happen."

She sank back until her head was against the seat rest and closed her eyes. Her hands were clenched so tightly now, her nails were digging into her palms. She didn't care if Ethan saw it or not. "And that's a final amount?" she managed to ask.

"No," he said and she opened her eyes, twisting to look at him. But before she could let the hope that was sputtering to life grow in her, he cut it off. "It's just what I said, a conservative guess, but the land isn't for sale to anyone."

"Are you sure?"

He shrugged. "Morgan, the plans are in the works. The financing's being set, and construction will begin in June, if they stay on schedule."

"Then they'll tear down the house and offices in June no matter what?"

"In all likelihood."

She grabbed at anything she could think of. "What if they find another place for the development?"

"That won't happen."

"But, if they did, then they could—"

He didn't let her go down that road. "They won't. That land is prime real estate, and to be honest, I'm concerned that no one in planning and development didn't see the potential until now."

Business. That was all he was concerned about. "If you had your way, we would have been thrown out a lot sooner."

"You're not being thrown out," he insisted. "The lease is up. It's that simple."

"Yeah, that simple," she said, knowing that finding another place was a logical next step, but setting up a medical office took time, and where would she and her dad work while they were doing that? Her father couldn't do it alone, either. Even if he hadn't talked about retiring, he couldn't manage and still help his patients. "Thanks for being honest with me," she said as disappointment crushed her.

"Listen, look for something else and let it go."

She probably should, but she couldn't. It was her home. It

meant so much to her and her father—and the islanders, too. "Do you really enjoy doing this?" When she heard herself ask the question she cringed. She was doing it again.

"I was brought up to learn that business is business. My father and my grandfather made the company what it is today. There's no way I'll undermine that."

"I know, I know, and pirating was Bartholomew's business. He did it quite well, like you do. From what I've heard and read, he took great joy in destroying things, and the bottom line was the gold he finally got."

She didn't expect Ethan to lean toward her, or to capture her chin with his hand. The touch wasn't hard, but it wasn't gentle, either. "If you're saying that's how I am, I don't know. I know I build things. I try to do positive things. What you have to understand is that sometimes the old needs to be removed to make way for the new."

She swallowed every response that rushed into her mind, and bit her lip to keep her silence. Ethan brushed her cheek. She was crying, and she hadn't realized it until he touched the wetness on her face. She didn't cry. She wouldn't cry. She sniffed and tried to stop the tears, but even as she did, Ethan blurred more in front of her.

"This isn't what I want," he said in a whisper as he gently stroked her cheek. "Believe me. It's not."

It wasn't what she wanted, either, but she was quite certain he wasn't having the same impulse she was at that moment. She had the crazy idea that if she held Ethan, things would be right, that the weight lying so heavily on her shoulders would lighten. *Wishful thinking,* she told herself and moved to get away from his touch, to try to stop the crazy thoughts that were coming to her.

A rap sounded on Ethan's window, startling them both. Ethan turned and rolled down the window to find James. He ducked down to look in the car. "Just wondering if you needed help." He flicked his gaze from Ethan to Morgan and hesitated. "Or maybe I should just…?"

"No," Morgan said quickly. "I need to get home."

Ethan was watching her, she could feel it, but she didn't glance in his direction. "Thanks," she heard him say, then he grabbed his crutch and got out. She waited just long enough for both men to step away from the car and head to the side door before she drove off. She didn't look in the rearview mirror or wipe the tears off her face until she was through the gates and off the Grace property.

She was all the way home before she finally felt able to breathe again. Climbing out into the chill of the foggy night, she hurried to the veranda and went inside. The remnants of the dinner were still on the table, but she ignored them. Tomorrow morning would be soon enough to clean up the mess. She needed to deal with something more important than dirty dishes. Heading back to the study, she got online on her father's computer. She did a search for Ethan's corporation and found the home page for the E.P.G. Corporation. Flashy and expensive-looking, it screamed prosperity and sleek power.

After several minutes, she got to the section on developments in planning and progress, and finally found what she was afraid she'd find. The page had a beautiful picture of the island, looking like a gem in the deep blue sound, under a crystal-clear sky. The banner on the page told it all—Bartholomew Bay Development. Since there wasn't a Bartholomew Bay on the island, it had to be the name of the project that would swallow up the offices, the house and the land around them. *Unmatchable views. Unsurpassed luxury. Coming soon.* The contact addresses and numbers for information on investments in the development were listed at the bottom.

She rested her elbows on the table and sank her head into her hands. She was back at square one. She'd said the wrong things, done the wrong things. She'd tried, damn it, but she'd failed miserably.

"Why do you always fight with the man?" she muttered to herself. "Why?" She'd really thought she could be reasonable, that she'd approach him carefully, that she'd be able to change the direction of things. Instead, she felt like Bartholomew Grace must have felt on his last run when his ship had been blown up, the remains left on the bottom of the Pacific. She felt lost, without a dry place to stand.

She sat back, slowly lowered her hands and looked around the room. Her eyes were dry now, but the desperation hadn't lessened at all. She'd hung on to the hope that she could make this right, that they could buy the land, or stop the development somehow. But that hope was fading fast. She'd thought she could convince Ethan to see things her way, but she knew that wasn't ever going to happen. He wasn't a cold person, but he was focused. Business was business for Ethan, just as it had been for Bartholomew.

She stood and went to her bedroom. Stripping off her clothes, she got into bed, turned out the lights and lay there alone, unable to stop thinking. Her mind swirled in all directions but never landed on any kind of answer. Then she closed her eyes and Ethan's image came to her. Those dark eyes watching her, his touch on her, brushing at her tears.

She rolled onto her stomach and pressed her face into the pillow, but that didn't stop Ethan from lingering in her thoughts. It didn't stop her from going over and over those last few moments with him in her car. She realized that she'd thought he was going to kiss her. She hadn't let herself think about that before, but alone in her room she could admit it to herself. And, inevitably, she admitted something else, something that left her feeling shaken. She'd *wanted* him to kiss her.

FOR THREE DAYS Ethan didn't call Morgan, or go by her house, or look for her on the beach below his estate. He thought about her more than he wanted to. He hated the memory of her crying, and really wished that life were more simple. He lay in his bed at night, watching the fog roll in over the sound, and didn't dream when he fell asleep.

He worked every waking hour, got a lot done, but everything he and Morgan had discussed came back to him when he sat in the guest house at the bachelor party he'd thrown for Joe. Ethan, Joe and James were lingering over brandy after the others had left, and Ethan was feeling very mellow. It felt good just to sit around with friends, laughing, drinking, joking and sharing their lives for a few hours. It wasn't complicated, and he welcomed a few hours, enjoying himself. Then Joe brought up Ethan's lack of Christmas decorations.

"You need to pay someone to put up a tree and some lights. You wouldn't even know it's Christmas around here."

James had been silent until then, sitting on the hearth, forming a triangle with Ethan on one couch, Joe on the other. "You tell him. He won't listen to me." He waved his hand around the room. "Not even a sprig of mistletoe."

"Fine by me," Ethan murmured. "I sure wouldn't want to get caught under that stuff with you close by."

Joe chuckled, and James said, "No way. I was thinking you and Natalie…or maybe the pretty doctor. I bet you wouldn't mind mistletoe if she was around."

Joe eyed Ethan. "You and Morgan? I wondered what was going on when you showed up at the house with her. But I had so much on my mind, I didn't think to ask."

"There's nothing to ask about," Ethan said, shifting his cast so he could grab the brandy decanter and splash more of the amber liquid in his snifter.

"I heard a rumor around town, that they were getting put out of their offices. I don't know who'd do that to them. Dr. Kelly's been here forever, and I don't know what everyone would do if he closed up shop."

"What would the locals do?" James asked with a bit of a slur in his tone. "Got any ideas who'd kick the doctor out of his offices?"

Ethan swirled the brandy in his snifter, watching the overhead lights catch in the dark liquid. James was really beginning to annoy him. "How about you go on the unemployment rolls?" he muttered.

"You're going to throw me out, too, boss?"

"Oh, no, Ethan, tell me it isn't so," Joe said.

He looked over at his friend. "No one's getting kicked out. The lease is up, and there are plans for the land."

Joe sipped more brandy, then sighed when he met Ethan's gaze. "Merry Christmas, now get out?"

"Yeah, Merry Christmas and get out," James said, considerably less clearly than Joe.

"You're drunk," Ethan said to him.

"You're Scrooge," James countered as he clumsily got to his feet. "And I'm going to bed."

"Good, go," Ethan said, and watched the big man make his way toward the front door.

"Congratuway…congrats, Joe." He tossed the words over his shoulder, then went out and closed the door with a resounding slam as he left.

"You're really putting Doc Kelly out of his offices?" Joe asked when they were alone.

"The lease is up." Ethan didn't drink any more. The evening, which had been going so well, was starting to sour for him. "He was notified, and he has more than enough time to find other facilities."

"Odd," Joe said.

"It's business," Ethan explained.

"No, not that. Morgan being with you at our house. Why would you two be together if you're the enemy?"

Ethan adjusted his position, making sure to avoid the table leg with his cast. "I'm not the enemy. I said it's business, not anything personal."

"Now that's a joke. Not personal? Get a grip. It's damn personal."

Ethan closed his eyes and opened them quickly when he saw an image of Morgan sitting next to him in the car, the tears on her cheeks. "It wasn't meant to be."

"Does she buy that?"

"No," he said honestly. "She thought she could purchase the land from us and stop the development."

"She can't?" Ethan named the figure Jaye had given him, and Joe whistled softly. "I guess not. I don't know too many people who'd have that kind of money lying around. Certainly not Dr. Kelly."

"Can we change the subject?" Ethan asked, meaning it.

"Okay," Joe said. "Is Natalie going to come to the wedding?"

Natalie was so far from Ethan's thoughts that he had to try to focus to think about the answer. "She was, but I'm not sure now."

"Too bad."

"Yeah, too bad," Ethan echoed, not meaning it at all. It was over completely between him and Natalie. He'd call her and let her know. But their relationship hadn't been serious, so ending it hadn't been difficult. Ending things with Morgan wasn't so easy.

Joe put his glass on the table, then stood. "I need to get

going. With the new house and all the plans, Alegra's got her hands full." He stretched his hands over his head and yawned. "I told her I'd meet her at the new house before midnight." He glanced at the clock on the hearth. "I've got fifteen minutes, and as much as I've loved being here with you, I'm leaving."

"Go and see your fiancée." Ethan started to push to his feet, but Joe stopped him.

"Don't get up. I know the way out. Thanks for everything."

After Joe left, Ethan sat by himself until the clock showed almost one in the morning. By the time he got into bed, he thought he was ready just to sleep. But he was wrong. He was still awake at three o'clock and sitting up in bed, his back against the headboard. He stared out at the night, at the fog and darkness. Not a Christmas light or a holly wreath was in sight.

He liked it that way. At least he had. He remembered the tree at Morgan's, her decorating it and the less than elegant Christmas plates on her table. He wasn't sure if there'd been mistletoe at her house or not. She hadn't pointed it out, and he hadn't looked. And if there had been…? He was honest enough with himself to know if he and Morgan had been standing beneath a sprig of it, he wouldn't have hesitated kissing her.

He pushed himself lower in the bed, rested his sore leg on the pillows he had stacked beneath it and tried to relax. But his thoughts hadn't stopped at just kissing Morgan. He was inundated by images of her leaning over him, touching him, and his body responded of its own volition. He reached to turn out the light, settled under the sheets, and gave up trying not to think about Morgan Kelly.

"Damn it," he muttered and punched the mattress beside him. He felt like a frustrated teenager, and he didn't have the option of jumping in his car and driving over to her house.

He lay flat on his back, rested his arm over his eyes and took several deep breaths. Tomorrow he'd figure out why he was acting like this, and why, when Morgan Kelly only wanted him around to talk him out of developing the property, he couldn't stop thinking about her.

Ethan slept sporadically and in between disturbing dreams he realized he might be able to help Morgan after all, and not compromise the business.

He was up at dawn, and by ten o'clock, he had the information he'd asked for. That was when he reached for the phone to call her. He got her nurse, Sharon, on the phone, and found out Morgan was out on an emergency. He left a message for her to call him when she could, then tried to work, but he found himself staring out the window at the rain, waiting for her call.

When the phone finally rang, he reached for it and heard Morgan on the other end of the line, her voice a bit breathless as if she'd been running. "Ethan, it's Morgan. You wanted me to call you?"

"Yes, I did. I wanted to make you an offer."

"An offer?" she said with a slight gasp.

He realized his mistake as soon as she spoke—she sounded excited, probably thinking he'd changed his mind, that maybe he'd called to tell her she could stay in the offices. He decided against any preamble and just stated what he'd call to say. "I'm offering to have my people look for other facilities for your offices on the island."

"Excuse me?" He'd been right. The excitement was gone, and she sounded downright disgusted.

"We could find something suitable and see about covering the relocation costs for you."

"Just a minute," she said. "Let me get this straight. You're offering to find a place for the offices and even help us relocate?"

"Yes, exactly. We have other properties on the island, and my staff would know of any that are either available now or coming up on the market."

He hadn't expected abject thankfulness on her part, but he didn't expect her abrupt "Why?"

Bad to worse. "Because I recognize that this is a huge inconvenience for you, and I'm just offering to help. If you don't want it, then—"

"Of course I'll take whatever help I can to make this work one way or another. But, honestly, if I found a place tomorrow, the idea that everything could be moved and set up by the time we have to vacate this place… It would be tight, and Dad couldn't do it alone. But if you can't cancel the project, maybe we could stay a bit longer at the old place. Another year would be doable."

She was actually still trying to negotiate with him. Tears or not, she hadn't given up. "That can't be done. The plans are in the works, permits obtained, money tied up for construction. Putting it off won't happen on any level."

"There's no way to postpone things?"

"Nothing short of a court order." He stopped when he realized what he was saying, then finished with, "It's on track and that's that."

She didn't let it pass. "So it could be challenged in court?"

He'd opened a can of worms. "Anything can be challenged in court, but all that does is cost both sides a lot of money."

He knew the Kellys didn't have funds to do that, but he was also quite certain that if Morgan got an idea in her head, she'd move heaven and earth to make it work. "But if we challenge the eviction and the proposed use of the land, what then?"

He was tired of feeling so miserly around her. "First of all, it's not an eviction and you'd have to come up with a compelling reason why the land shouldn't be developed. I can assure you, there are no issues with this project."

"That you know of."

"There absolutely aren't," he countered, and he knew he'd spoken too quickly when she laughed softly.

"One thing you learn from practicing medicine is there are very few absolutes except death."

He closed his eyes. The woman on the other end of the phone was absolutely infuriating, and yet so absolutely intriguing. He'd thought by now she'd be thanking him, saying she would gladly accept his help and maybe, just maybe, he would get to see her smile again. Instead, he was in a war of words with her. "I just wanted to make the offer," he said, then finished with another offer. "If you're interested, let me know when you're free to look at properties and we'll do it."

She didn't reply, and he did what he never did in business when he was anxious to close a deal or come to terms with a competitor—he spoke before he got their response. "Do want to do this or not?"

He heard her sigh, then speak in a softer tone. "Sure, I'll do it. I'll look. It'll be fine. It'll work." He released a breath he hadn't been aware he was holding. "Okay, sure, but I have to get back to work," she said.

He looked out the window, then glanced down at the fax in front of him. "Call me when you can get away."

"I'll call," she said, then took him by surprise by saying, "Thank you, Ethan," before she hung up.

He sat alone in the office, rocking back and forth and hoping that they'd find the perfect place for her father. Then they really could start fresh. Just as a man and a woman. He couldn't quite figure out why that had become so important to him.

James had always told Ethan that if they walked into a

room, he could pick out the one woman Ethan would be attracted to. "Flashy, high-powered and stunning."

Morgan wasn't high-powered and there was nothing really flashy about her, except for her hair color. Her slender figure under simple clothes was nice. She wasn't particularly stunning, until she smiled. She'd had him with her smile, and he wanted to see her smile again.

Chapter Nine

At four-thirty that afternoon, Morgan walked out of a building that had, at one time, been an automotive-repair place, and headed for Ethan's SUV, which was idling on the pothole-riddled parking lot. The tinted windows almost hid the man who was sitting in the passenger seat.

Less than an hour after he'd offered to help find a new location for the clinic, she'd called him back, saying she was free. She'd agreed to go to Ethan's house, get the list of places from him and look at them on her own, but when she'd arrived, James was ready to chauffeur them around the island. She'd stopped that idea immediately, but no matter what she said, Ethan had insisted on coming with her. They'd compromised by having her drive Ethan's car so he had room for his injured leg, and James had stayed at home since he was nursing a hangover from last night's bachelor party.

She climbed back behind the wheel of the SUV, pushed her damp hair off her face and closed the door on the late-afternoon cold air. "It won't work," she said as she put the car in gear and drove away from the brick building.

"Why not?"

The windshield wipers came on automatically, and Morgan stared straight ahead at the rain-slick road. "The square footage is doable, but the location is too far from town and parking is short. Besides, the plumbing would have to be completely redone, along with the wiring, and it would be really time-consuming and costly to bring it all up to code. And it's a lease, so we'd be right back where we started in five years. We need to buy so that won't happen again."

Ethan shifted in his seat, but didn't speak. When she glanced at him, he seemed intent on the road ahead of them. He was in his bomber jacket, dark pants and a white shirt. His hair was damp from the rain, and he seemed oddly distracted. It had been his idea to do this, now he seemed to be in another place.

She brushed at her hair that was fast becoming an unruly halo of wild curls from the humidity. "I think maybe I should only look at places close to town with ample parking and that already have updated plumbing and electrical service. We can strike out anything that's for lease or for rent."

Ethan made a low sound to let her know he'd heard her, but otherwise kept silent.

"Are there any locations on the list that fit that criteria?"

He moved, and she heard paper rustle. "No."

"Then I guess I'll take you back home."

"No," he said again, and she stared at him. He was studying her now, a frown drawing his dark brows together. "Not yet."

She pulled to the side of the road about a half mile from the northern edge of town, put the car in Park, and as the rain increased from a light drizzle to a downpour, she twisted in the seat to look at him. His eyes met hers as his fingers tapped rapidly on his thigh. She knew he'd gone to some trouble to get the list of properties—why, she still didn't quite understand, although she appreciated it—but she was no closer to finding an answer to her troubles than she'd been when they had started.

"If we don't have any more properties to look at, what else is there to do?" she asked.

Ethan dropped his head back against the headrest and closed his eyes. He pinched the bridge of his nose and didn't answer her. He'd insisted on coming along, but he seemed more and more distracted as they drove. Now he just looked pained.

"What's wrong?" she finally said.

He dropped his hand to his thigh and sat a bit straighter. Rain beat down on the car, but her whole attention was on Ethan. "I need to ask you something."

She braced herself. "Okay," she said. "What?"

"I know this whole building situation is hard on you, and that it's pretty damn important to you and your father."

That was a given. "Of course it is."

He studied her intently from under lowered lids, then asked, "Why did you feel you had to go around telling everyone that I'm kicking you and your family out of your home and business offices?"

She blinked at him and knew there was more than a bit of anger in his expression now. "Me? I haven't told anyone." She'd thought about telling her father, but hadn't wanted to add to his worries. She wanted answers, to find a way to fix the mess that was going to fall on them come March.

"Then it doesn't figure. How could the whole town find out, and want to string me up to boot?"

"I promise, I never said a thing to…" She stopped when she realized that wasn't exactly true. "I told Sharon in the office because she saw the letter and—"

"This damn town," he muttered. "She told someone, and they told someone, and now I'm a minus zero on the likability scale."

He was upset because the town didn't like him? She had no idea he'd ever care what people around here thought about him. In some way that endeared him to her on a whole new level. He cared about the people around here. He wasn't cold-hearted and ready to bulldoze over everyone. "I'm sorry that happened."

"Gossip around here is almost its own industry," he said.

That was true. Gossip was rampant, but it wasn't always bad. It stemmed from concern most of the time. But this time, she could tell it really wounded Ethan. "How did you find out that people knew?"

He shrugged. "After I talked to you, I got three calls at the house from locals who wanted to ask me about my shameful dealings with you and your dad. One went so far as to tell James that I was old Bartholomew personified." Ethan held up a hand immediately to stop any response from her. "I know how you feel," he said. "I just had no idea the stigma of the pirate was so strong with this generation."

"If you were around here more, you'd find out that most townspeople actually are proud of the pirate. Not what he did to others, but his determination to stay here and build roots on the island."

He chuckled at that. "Oh sure, proud of some blood-thirsty pirate who probably forced a few of his ancestors to walk the plank or worse."

"That's possible, but who's to say they didn't deserve a watery grave?"

That brought a real laugh from the man next to her, and the sound gave her a glimpse of what Ethan must have been like before he went out to conquer the world. "I can't argue with that," he finally said.

She couldn't look away from him. In the past few minutes, she'd seen more of the man she thought was the real Ethan Grace than she had in the days she'd known him. But getting that glimpse of who she thought he might be—or could be— only intensified her discomfort at being in such close quarters with him. She'd already admitted to herself that he was attractive, but the longer she stayed in here with him, the more she found herself wanting him. Words such as *sexy* and *handsome* came to mind even though he didn't look anything like a pretty boy.

She took a breath, but found she couldn't get too much air into her lungs. "I'll just have to tell anyone who will listen that you're helping me, and that you're a great guy."

"Don't go to that extreme," he said as his smile deepened with a degree of self-deprecation. "Just tell them I'm not an ogre."

Not even close to an ogre, she thought, but simply said, "You've got it." She needed to get fresh air, as well as put some space between herself and the man who was making her realize she could so easily do a lot more than just like Ethan Grace. She felt a fire in her that didn't have a thing to do with the heater in the car, and she turned away from Ethan to put the car in Drive.

When she closed her hand over the gearshift, Ethan covered her hand with his, stopping her. She held her breath, but didn't attempt to break the contact. "Hold on. I just had an idea. There's a property that's not on the list, but it's got the square footage and plenty of room for parking and future expansion."

"You own it?" she asked, her thoughts not entirely clear with him touching her.

"The company has an interest in it."

"Where is it?"

"In town proper." He released her hand to motion ahead of them. "Come on. I'll show it to you."

She drove into town, the rain and wind causing the stoplights strung across the street to sway. When they were within a block of the medical offices, Ethan told her to turn right on a short and narrow side street away from the water.

The road dead-ended at a sprawling expanse of vacant

land that flowed back in the distance to a thick forest. Morgan had been to the place before years ago. There was nothing she could see that would be appropriate for what she needed, and she pulled the car to a stop where the pavement ran into mud on the bare land.

The house to their right had been owned by the Payne family. She'd heard their only son Sean, who had become a local celebrity for his artwork, lived there off and on now. There wasn't a For Sale sign anywhere. To the left stood a three-story Victorian, one of the original homes on the island. But unlike similar homes on the main street that had been restored and turned into pricy bed-and-breakfasts or upscale shops, this house had been empty for a very long time and obviously neglected. Its gingerbread trim had partly fallen off, the wooden roof shingles were green with moss and several were missing. The windows were covered in grime, and the steps to the wraparound porch sagged to the right.

She looked from house to house, then to Ethan. "What did you think would be perfect?"

He waved at the land directly ahead of them. "That piece of land. Since you have to start all over basically, why not build exactly what you want?"

She stared at the empty lot and felt her chest tighten at the idea of what could be done with the property. An acre at least, there would be room for the office complex and the clinic with tons of parking. But the excitement faded quickly. "Nice daydream," she murmured.

"The location's near what you wanted. No view, but lots of space. And you could build from the ground up and have it the way you want it right from the start."

"It would be wonderful, but it would take so much time to construct, even a basic setup, and the money…" She exhaled. "It would cost a fortune."

She realized the rain had let up, and mist swirled in the air. "Let's get out of the car and at least take a good look."

Taking a better look wouldn't change a thing, and a part of her didn't want to start imagining what could be. It couldn't be done, at least not by her and her dad.

She didn't make a move to open the door, even when Ethan had his open and was swinging his injured leg out. He glanced at her when he reached for the crutch. "Coming?"

Fresh air might help her clear her head and her thoughts, so she nodded and got out. By the time she walked around to Ethan, he was leaning against the hood of the SUV and surveying the land. "I remember being here years ago," he said as if talking to himself.

She stood by his side and leaned back, echoing his stance. Crossing her arms over her chest for some protection against the cold, she studied the property. "I've been to the Paynes', before Sean became anything more than a pain in the neck."

Ethan chuckled at that. "I hear he's still a major pain, but now it's called a 'creative temperament.'" He motioned to the land. "So, what do you think?"

"It definitely has potential, but as I said, we don't have the time or the funds to do something like this." She scrubbed a hand over her face and sighed, partly from weariness and partly from frustration. "I don't know what to do."

There was silence all around them, then Ethan broke it with a touch and words. His hand slipped around her shoulders, and he spoke softly to her. "Do what you have to do to make it work," he said. "Just do it."

She turned, but he didn't let her go, and she was so close to him that she felt his body heat radiating to her cool face. "Now, that sounds like a commercial."

He smiled, a slow, soft expression and it made her heart lurch. "Even if it is, it's the way to get through life."

"Is that how you manage life?" she asked. "You just do it and it works out?"

He lifted his other hand and brushed her cheek with a feathery touch that brought more heat with it. "To be honest, a lot of things haven't worked out for me," he said just above a whisper. "But I try, and if I mess up, I have myself alone to blame. No one else."

She felt much the same right then. The decisions were hers to make right now—and to fail at, if they didn't work out. But her decisions would affect her father and the whole island. The weight of responsibility was heavy on her, and she felt incredibly alone. She'd had the same feeling treating her patients, knowing her choices would affect the rest of their lives.

Ethan tightened his hold on her, and for that single moment in time, she didn't feel alone. She felt connected. She couldn't remember feeling like this before, and she couldn't remember ever wanting just to cling to someone before, either.

That shook her, and she pulled out of his embrace, saying something generic like, "Sure, of course," that said nothing really. But he let her go, and she felt the isolation down to her soul. It took all she had not to reach out and let him hold her again. "Just do it," she said as she went to get into the car again.

WHEN MORGAN MOVED AWAY from Ethan, the cold came back to him full force. He watched her go to the car, reach for the handle, then she drew back. She turned to look at him, then at the old Victorian house. She stood there as if studying the place. "Do you have a flashlight?"

"I don't know. If there is one, it's probably in the glove compartment."

She opened the driver's door and ducked inside. Moments later she had a large flashlight in her hand. She snapped it on, said, "I'll be right back," and jogged toward the old house. The beam of light danced crazily with each step she took, showing the sagging stairs that she took in two strides, then exposing the front door as she approached it.

"What are you doing?" he called, aware of a few drops of rain that touched his face.

"Going inside to look around," she shouted to him.

"Why?"

"Why not?" she called.

He watched her disappear inside and waited for all of a minute as rain started to come down faster before he reached for his crutch and headed after her. He had to take the broken walkway to keep the crutch from sinking into the mud all around, and finally made it to the open front door. He shook himself to try to clear some of the clinging rain, then entered the darkness.

He caught the smell of must and mold, and found himself in a large square space that he guessed had been the formal foyer at one time in the past. "Morgan?"

"Hold on." Her voice came from the rear of the house. Light flashed through the door right ahead of him. He caught the suggestion of a long hallway in the glow, then Morgan spoke. "I just thought that maybe this could work."

"But it's older than dirt and it's not fixed."

"Sure it's old and not kept, but I remembered that when I was a kid, this place was a boarding house. So it had to have good plumbing and electricity to support a lot of people living in it. It's got lots of space, and if you go down the hallway, there are at least six rooms off of it. They could be examination rooms. The living room could be for waiting, and its location is great. On top of that, the whole third floor could be living quarters for my dad." She spoke rapidly as if high on excitement.

"It's a mess," he said, as his eyes adjusted to the lack of light. He could see peeling wallpaper and dust everywhere.

"You said to be creative, and I'm trying. There's the land by it, and eventually, if we could get the money, it could be a good spot for extra parking and the clinic."

He'd told her to just do it, and she seemed to be taking his advice, but he didn't share her enthusiasm. The place was almost falling down. "It's old, and even if it was up to code when you were a child, it certainly wouldn't be today."

He looked at her, her features smudged by shadows, but he could tell that his words had hit their mark. The excitement drained from her, and he could see reality setting in. "You're right," she whispered. "Stupid of me."

He didn't think it would work, either, but he hated to hear the creeping defeat in her voice and felt guilty for being the cause of it. She was very still, a soft shadow among so much shadow. He heard her breathing, shallow and rapid, and he had the feeling she was holding back tears. He knew how upside down his emotions had become since meeting Morgan Kelly when he had a passing thought that, if he could—even if it meant a huge loss for the company—he'd let her keep her damn offices and house.

He didn't know where the idea came from, but he rejected it out of hand. It was ridiculous and suicidal for the company. *Don't let emotion come into business.* He'd given that advice to a lot of people, especially to Morgan. Now he was doing it. "No, it wasn't stupid," he assured her. "You just need to keep looking."

"Sure," she said, her tone flat now. "My dad isn't back until after New Year's, so that gives me a couple of weeks. There has to be something around here that I can make work."

Her voice was soft in the semidarkness, and he moved closer to her. "Morgan, we can keep looking."

"No." The single word hung between them. "I'll do it. You're…"

"I'm what?" he asked.

"I don't know." She released a sob suddenly, the sound almost lost in the cavernous old house. Lightning flashed everywhere, and for a split second, he saw Morgan. There was no color, just her huge eyes and a decidedly stricken look on her face. Then thunder rumbled across the heavens, and she dropped the flashlight to the ground, its beam cutting through the darkness at crazy angles.

"Oh, damn it," Morgan gasped, and she fell to her haunches to grab the light, only to knock it farther away. She finally just let it go, slowly stood and, without a word, Ethan reached out to her.

He didn't know if she'd let him touch her or if she'd pull away. She simply stood there, and when his crutch slipped to the floor, neither one paid any attention to the clatter. Ethan's focus was on Morgan alone, and he caught her to him, folding her into his arms. He felt her trembling, and then her hands moved slowly around his waist, and her face pressed into his chest. When more thunder struck, she jerked, then held more tightly to him.

"Thunder scares you?" he asked, very aware of the way the curves of her body fit neatly against him.

"No, not thunder," she whispered, then eased back enough to look up at him. "It's this whole mess. I mean…"

The idea of kissing Morgan came in a flash akin to lightning, but it didn't die out. He lowered his head and touched her lips with his. He felt heat and unsteadiness, then he pulled her closer to him. Her hips pressed to his, and her lips parted under the demands of his mouth.

He tasted her and shifted his hands, splaying them across her back, keeping her close to him. He felt connected to her in a way he couldn't begin to comprehend, and that only made him want more of her. He wanted to understand her, to know why this woman drew him like a moth to flame. She strained against him, almost frantic in her actions, and he echoed the same urgency. Her hands were working their way under his jacket, then tugging at his shirt.

Skin touched skin, her palms against his naked chest. He moved her back awkwardly, catching her between his body and the wall. He pushed aside her jacket, then pulled up the soft wool of her sweater. Splaying his fingers on her taut stomach, he heard her gasp sharply at the contact. His touch went higher, finding the thin lace of her bra, and feeling her hard, aroused nipples under the flimsy covering. He caught one between his forefinger and thumb and was gratified to hear her soft moan in his ears. His lips tasted her jaw, then the spot below her ear and the hollow of her throat.

He'd expected a kiss. He'd wanted a kiss. But that kiss had exploded between them. He could feel his arousal straining against his pants and the way her body arched into his. Nothing mattered but being closer to her, touching her, having her. Her lips found his throat, then moved up, and she nibbled at his earlobe. The guttural groan he heard was his, and he tugged at her bra, releasing her breasts from the lace. She was all silk and heat, and it filled him. The essence of her was everywhere, and he wanted her more than he'd ever wanted anyone in his life.

"What in the hell?" someone yelled through the maze of emotions and darkness. Ethan froze.

A beam of light cut into the house, missing them by five feet, and Ethan felt like a teenager caught at a makeout point. He looked at Morgan, standing so close to her that only a few inches separated their mouths, and he saw the horror in her eyes. She pushed him away, freeing herself from his grasp. She frantically pulled at her sweater to get it back into place.

Ethan moved back, but didn't turn away from her. He took

his time adjusting his clothes, although there was no way he could hide the physical evidence of what had just happened, or at least, almost happened.

"You in there," the voice shouted again, and this time the light was closer, swinging to the right. As Ethan turned, it caught the two of them in its penetrating beam.

Ethan blinked at it, putting up his forearm to shield himself from the glare, then he heard the person behind the light say with obvious shock. "Holy cow. Doc Kelly, is that you?"

Morgan had stayed behind Ethan, but she barely brushed the sleeve of his jacket as she came to his side. "Darren, is that you?" she asked.

The light lowered and that was when Ethan saw a middle-aged man dressed in a dark slicker and hat that were dripping from the rain. Ethan knew Darren Appleby. He had been on the island for as long as Ethan could remember. He did odd jobs, disappearing for long periods of time to the mainland, but he always came back.

He stooped to pick up the long-forgotten flashlight near his feet, then straightened and came to hold it out to the two of them. Morgan quickly took it and clicked it off.

"Yeah, Doc, it's me. What are you all doing in—?" His voice cut off when his light flashed on Ethan. "Oh, man, it's you," he said to Ethan. "They pay me to keep an eye on this place, and I saw the car, then the light. I came to check it out and never thought I'd see you in here, much less with Dr. Kelly."

Before either one could respond, Darren kept talking. "What're you doing with this guy? There he is, going to put you and your dad on the street and you're here with him. I don't get it."

One more person who obviously wanted Ethan strung up or walking the plank. "That's not any of your business," Ethan said, and he knew it was the wrong thing to say when the other man all but exploded at him.

Darren pointed the light straight at Ethan, blinding him for a moment. "What's my business is that you're taking over the whole section on the water, and that includes the offices where her daddy started and has been for most of my life. That ain't right."

Ethan had had enough of this. He felt like a punching bag for the people around here. "Get that light out of my eyes," he said, and the beam dropped to his feet immediately, but that didn't help matters.

Darren saw the cast and spoke with dripping sarcasm. "Broke something? Maybe you need a doctor. Too bad you won't be able to find one around here in the future."

Ethan exhaled, barely controlling his growing irritation. "It's just business," he muttered and knew it was the wrong thing to say once again.

"Business?" Darren bit out. "I'll give you—"

"Darren!" Morgan said, derailing what would have been another tirade against Ethan. "How did you find out what's happening with Dad's place?"

He waved the hand holding the flashlight and the beam cut through the darkness in a crazy arc before coming back to rest at Morgan's feet. "Someone caught a big promo on the Internet for 'Bartholomew's Cove.' Fancy schmancy stuff. Just floored us. Your poor dad. He must be going crazy with his life and good work for the islanders going down the toilet because of—"

"Darren. Dad doesn't know, not yet," Morgan said quickly.

"Good enough. He deserves to relax for a while. But what are you going to do about all of this?"

"I don't know yet, but I'm working on it."

"Don't let him push you around." He sneered at Ethan.

Ethan hadn't expected hostility like this. It wasn't as if he was tearing up the island and destroying its character. He glanced at Morgan, who was all but lost in the thick shadows of the house. But he could see her hands, and they were in tight fists. "I'm taking care of things."

"Okay, good enough for now," Darren said, putting the flashlight square in Ethan's face again. "Don't be pushing her around," he repeated, then left.

Ethan grumbled. "The whole damn town has it all wrong."

"What did he get wrong?" Morgan asked after a pause.

When they'd been together, Ethan hadn't felt any barriers, but in that moment, when he turned to her, a very large barrier stood between them. "Have I been pushing you around?"

"We should get out here."

"Give me the damn flashlight," he said, and Morgan held it out to him. He snapped it on as his anger rose, along with a huge dose of frustration on every level imaginable. He spotted the crutch, picked it up, then stepped out under the protection of the porch roof. The storm beat down with torrential rain and Ethan felt pummeled himself. But not from the elements, from a woman, the woman he had come very close to making love with.

Chapter Ten

Morgan couldn't even look at Ethan now, let alone touch him again, not after what she'd let happen inside. She'd never been fond of Darren, seeing him mostly as a drifter who did little that was productive, but in this one instance, she'd been glad he showed up when he did. If he hadn't, she didn't know how far she would've gone. She stopped at the top of the stairs, just barely under the protection of the roof, and stared out at the rain.

No, she knew what would have happened, even in the old, dank house. She knew too well, and the thought made her unsteady. She wrapped her arms around herself, and spoke to Ethan without turning to him. "Do we wait this out or just take our chances?"

She heard his crutch thump on the wooden floor as he came closer. "I'll take my chances."

She closed her eyes, hoping against hope that he wouldn't touch her again, but she need not have worried about it. He never made any contact with her. "You'll be soaked by the time you get to the car."

"I won't melt." He was inches behind her.

"Is that a fiberglass cast?"

"Hell, I don't know."

"If it's not, it'll dissolve," she said.

She wasn't sure how she thought he'd react to what they'd done in the house, but hadn't expected him to be cold and distant. Then again, maybe that was a favor to her. Then she wouldn't have to stop him from kissing her again, or walk away from his touch. One kiss and she'd melted. Reason had fled to some dark corner where she hadn't been able to find it. "I'll take my chances," he said a second time.

"Okay," she said on a sigh. "I'll get the car and bring it as close as I can."

"Then you'll get soaked."

"I'm not wearing a cast," she shot back at him right before she plunged down the stairs into the stormy night. She ran across the lawn, the rain pelting down, almost tripping at one point, but catching herself just in time. She made it to the big car, got inside, and didn't worry about dripping water on the leather interior.

She ran a hand over her wet hair, pushing it back from her face as best she could, then started the engine and drove toward the house. She'd thought she'd stop at the end of the broken walkway that led to the porch steps, but forced the SUV onto the wet grass. Although the tires started to sink, they never lost traction.

She got near the porch, catching Ethan in the headlights. He was watching her, and she noticed that his shirt was still untucked, the bottom buttons undone. Her mouth went dry at the thoughts that came to her, then she turned left, swinging the lights off of the man and coming to a stop. She waited, saw Ethan adjust his crutch then start down the steps.

He moved as quickly as he could, but by the time he was at the door, which she'd opened for him, his hair was plastered to his head and his shirt, where his jacket parted, stuck to his chest like a second skin. "Hurry," she said. He was inside, pushing his crutch into the backseat, in less than a minute.

He closed the door, then sat back. "Damn if you weren't right," he muttered as he ran his fingers through his drenched hair, spiking it around his face. "Soaked to the bone."

Morgan knew she wasn't much better off than him. She felt cold water running under her collar and down her back. Her jacket felt heavy across her shoulders, and her hair would be a curly mess as soon as it began to dry.

"Oh, damn," he muttered.

"What is it?" she asked as put the car in gear and made a wide arc back over the lawn and out onto the street.

"You were right," he admitted grudgingly. "There's water under the cast."

She headed down the short street, which now looked like a small river flowing toward the main road. "That's not good," she said. If the cast were weakened, it could fail and do a lot more damage to his already injured leg. With the heavy rain, she was sure the ferry would stop running and flying a helicopter would be out of the question. So his doctor certainly wasn't going to show up to recast his leg. Knowing there wasn't much else to do, she didn't turn north as she'd intended to take him back the Grace estate. Instead, she headed south toward her offices.

"Wrong direction," he said, when he realized where they were going.

"I'll take you to the clinic and see what the cast is made of and if I can get the moisture out of it."

"You're giving the enemy aid?" he asked.

She slowed as she neared the office parking area. The enemy? That was a joke. He might be her opponent, but she was quite sure that the way she'd responded to him a short time ago certainly wiped out any reason for her to call him the enemy. "A doctor treats those who need treatment, no questions asked," she said, and realized how prim that sounded. "In other words, I just do it."

She knew he was watching her as she swung left after a car passed, and drove by the front parking and the lights in the window that spelled out *Merry Christmas*. She went to a side entrance off an old car port that was good protection from the downpour. The big SUV barely cleared the aluminum roof as she came to a stop.

"Just do it?" Ethan asked.

"Sorry for that. It still sounds like a commercial," she said as she got out. She had the office keys in her hand before she reached the door and opened it to quickly step inside. Leaving it ajar, she turned on the lights. Being in the car with Ethan had unnerved her, but as she looked around the decoration-saturated waiting room, she wondered if it would be any easier inside.

She heard the door shut behind her, and didn't turn to look at Ethan. She pulled off her jacket and hung it on a wall hook by the entrance that led to the examination rooms. "Get your jacket off, if you want to," she said as she went through the first door.

She flipped on the light and the glare of the intense overhead fixture flooded the room. Unlike the main room, there was nothing festive in here, just green walls, white cabinets with a sink, a metal examination table topped with a thick white pad and supplies stacked on a floor-to-ceiling shelf unit next to a sterilization unit.

There was just enough room for the two of them when Ethan appeared at the door. He'd taken off his jacket and his damp shirt was clinging to every place it made contact, outlining his chest and toned arms. She was inordinately grateful to have work to do. Staring at him only made her remember how it felt to touch him and feel his heart hammer against her palms.

Now the room seemed almost suffocating to her. She left the door open and motioned to the exam table. "Can you get up there?"

"Sure," he said, leaning his crutch against the wall before maneuvering himself up and onto the table. That brought him eye to eye with Morgan, and she had an impulse to brush at the damp hair that clung to his forehead. But she didn't. Instead, she pulled out a support shelf and helped him lift his injured leg onto it. She concentrated on what she was doing as she tugged back the leg of his slacks and checked the cast.

Very little water had actually managed to get into it at the top, but the bottom was worse for the wear where it had made contact with the sodden ground. "Well, it's not fiberglass, although I can't imagine why it isn't. However, the top's fine, but I think I should cut some off around your heel and redo it," she said, tugging at the wet, ruined fiber in the cast. "It's falling apart there and that weakens the total support." She looked up and met Ethan's gaze. "Is it okay with you if I try to repair it?"

"You're the doctor."

"Yes, I am the doctor," she said and reached for a pair of latex gloves. She got out the plaster bandage, knife and scissors, then started to work. For ten minutes, she felt Ethan watching her as she carefully stripped off the material. She cut away any compromised bandage, integrating the new bandages with the old materials. Finally when she was finished, she studied her work. It didn't look perfect, but it would do. She stripped off her gloves and tossed them in the trash. "Done," she said.

"Nice work," Ethan said.

"Simple cast repair 101," she said and cleaned up, putting

away the supplies and wiping down the counter. "Just keep it dry and don't put any pressure on it until it's totally set."

Ethan got down off the table and reached for his crutch. "I appreciate this. Just send me the bill."

She shook her head. "There's no charge."

"I can see why you aren't flaming rich," he said, hooking his arm over the crutch and found his balance.

"I never wanted to be 'flaming rich,' just comfortable."

He grimaced. "Of course. Flaming rich is so decadent, isn't it?"

"Is it?"

"Okay, I deserved that, but between you and me, I'm not flaming rich. Just very, *very* comfortable."

"If you say so," she murmured and noticed the way he was looking around the room, taking in its obvious lack of pretension on any level.

"You know, I thought from the way you're fighting everything, that this would be…different."

"It's perfect for what it is." She shrugged, and felt her damp sweater tug on her skin. "Repairing a cast isn't exactly brain surgery," she said at the same time her cell phone in her jacket pocket rang. The sound was muffled and distant, but she heard it clearly. "Dr. Kelly," she said after retrieving the phone.

"Mr. Apollo Walls called and needs to know if you said to take two pills once a day, or one pill twice a day, and how far apart he should take them if it's one twice a day, or when to take them if it's two, once a day." Vonya Dale, the lady who operated her call service, chuckled at what she'd just said. "Well, that's just about as convoluted a question as I've ever tried to relay."

"Give it to me again," Morgan said, aware of Ethan walking into the waiting room. While Vonya repeated the message,

Morgan turned off the light in the examination room, then went back to the waiting area. Ethan was standing by the Christmas tree, fingering one of the paper chains draped on it.

"And that's as much as I can tell you. What's he supposed to do about his medication?"

"Tell Mr. Walls to take one capsule four times a day, four hours apart."

"Got it. I'll get right back to him, unless you want to make the call."

"No, you can do it," Morgan said and hung up. Ethan, still by the tree, was leaning on his crutch. The shirt clung to his back, showing his muscles tense when he shifted his foot. She averted her gaze, then said, "That's done."

"Was that about Apollo Walls?"

"You know him?"

"Used to, years ago. He was having trouble taking his medicine?" he asked without looking away from the tree.

"The patient…" she said, without confirming if it was Apollo Walls or not. "He's a bit obsessive-compulsive, checks and double-checks everything, and then checks again."

"So he calls you for directions?"

"Not really. He calls for reassurance," she said and reached out to touch one of the popcorn balls that dangled from the tree's branches. "This is Sharon's area to decorate, and every year she brings in a tree from her place near the old lighthouse. She lives a bit inland, and they have the most beautiful pines on their property. She gets the kids to make the chains and do the balls." Morgan looked at the top of the tree where an angel made from silver and gold pipe cleaners clung to the highest branch. "Sharon made that angel and it's been on the top of every one of her trees for years."

Suddenly her eyes burned with tears and she ducked her head as she crouched and straightened some of the presents under the tree. Damn it, her emotions were on a roller coaster and she closed her eyes tight to get control.

"I don't get it," Ethan said. "This whole thing just doesn't make sense to me. You're insisting on having this place kept intact, but it seems to me that relocating could be a step up."

She opened her eyes and saw the closest present to her, a small box wrapped in Santa Claus paper, topped with a big green bow. A step up? It probably would be, she admitted to herself, but it wasn't about stepping up. It was about where they belonged, and where patients felt safe and cared for. It was what this place had become. It was where *she* felt safe and knew that, no matter what happened, it would always be here for her to come back to until she returned for good.

This was home. And she could finally say exactly why she was fighting to keep it. She wanted it to be here forever, for her and her father and the people who depended on them. She'd thought she'd been working to save the clinic for her dad and for the islanders, but all this time, it had been for her. She stood and turned to Ethan. "I'm not looking for a step up," she said. "This *is* my home. This is the reason for everything that I do and that my dad does. It's everything that I love."

"Then why did you leave to work in Seattle?" he asked.

That was a good question, because right then she knew it was time for her to be here permanently. "I guess I needed to do something on my own, maybe prove myself out there. But in the end…" She sighed. "This is where it all started, where dad helps our friends and neighbors. All this time I thought this place was ours. My dad never told me we didn't own it. I don't know why." She shivered and hugged herself. "But this land is our home, in the purest sense of the word. It's what we've put in to living here all these years." She stopped herself, not willing to expose any more of herself than she already had with this man. "Sorry, you wouldn't understand."

His dark eyes studied her, then he said, "You're right, I don't understand." He turned toward the rack that held their jackets. He got his, shook it out, then draped it over his arm. Realizing that was the end of the conversation, she ended up doing the same with hers; it was far too wet to put back on. She crossed to the door, pulled it open and absorbed the gust of damp, cold air that flooded into the office. She flipped off the light, then stood back to let Ethan leave first. As soon as he passed her, she went out, locked the door, then got onto the SUV.

They were in the car for at least five minutes on the drive to his house before he spoke again. Until then, she thought he'd written off the episode at the old house, but clearly she'd been mistaken. "So, why didn't you tell Darren the truth when he found us?"

She laughed, but it held no humor, just self-conscious nervousness. "What, that we were making out?"

"I didn't mean that. I was talking about him jumping on me for being the bad guy and you just standing there letting him rip me up one side and down the other. I'm not the enemy."

He'd long ago ceased being the enemy, and was perilously close to being something a great deal more disturbing to her than that. "You didn't need me to defend you."

Christmas decorations glowed through the rain, and the surrounding trees swayed in the growing wind. "But you do agree with Darren that I'm like Bartholomew. That's what you said yourself, didn't you?"

"I guess what I meant when I said it is you're totally focused on what you want, and that you don't think of the consequences."

"And if I did, what would I see and how would it change things?"

"I don't know what you'd see, I only know what I see."

"Which is?"

A man who stood between her and so much that she wanted. "People," she said vaguely. "Family, friends, patients. I consider them in anything I do or any decision I make."

She felt him shift, before he said, "Maybe you can do that, but I think it's a real mistake to let emotions get in the way or color your decisions."

"And you don't?"

"I damn well try not to."

"I don't know whether to congratulate you or offer you my sympathy."

He didn't respond and she didn't look over at him. She watched the rainy night all around them until she slowed and turned in at the closed gates of his estate. Before she could roll down the window to ask security for admittance, the gates started to open. "Wow, I'm impressed," she said.

"Don't be. There are cameras, and James has eyes in the back of his head. He sees all, knows all and can push a button with the best of them," Ethan said.

"I can't imagine that you pay him enough," she joked as she drove through the opening and headed for the main house.

"His very words," he said. "Every day."

"What's his title?" she asked as she made her way toward the portico over the side entrance where she'd dropped him before.

"I always say it's gofer, but he says it's executive facilitator and my friend."

She pulled to a stop under the protective roof and looked at Ethan in the low glow from the dash lights. His hair had started to curl slightly at his temples as it dried, and his eyes were lost in shadow. "Thanks for showing me the properties."

"Tell me something about tonight," he said without making a move to get out.

She groaned inwardly for thinking that she could leave without him wanting to discuss what happened between them this afternoon. "Listen, I'm sorry for what happened at the house, but well, I...it was the weather. I guess I hate thunder, and I get a bit crazy. And that house—good grief." She spoke in a rush, her words tumbling out one on top of the next. "I just was thankful that Darren didn't walk right in. I mean, he's such a gossip and already he'll be telling people that he found us there. That should make fodder for some interesting conjecture, but at least he can tell them nothing happened."

He held up a hand, palm out to her. "Whoa, stop. I wish you'd stop apologizing to me for everything, especially when I wasn't even talking about what you're apologizing for."

She'd done it again—assumed what he would say and put her foot in her mouth well and good. "Oh," she said, thankful he couldn't see the color she knew was flooding her cheeks. It only deepened when she tagged on a monumental lie. "Because it really was nothing. It just happened, and it...was nothing."

"Sure, nothing," he echoed.

A rap on the passenger side window startled her, and James opened the door and ducked down to look inside. He glanced at her, then at his boss with a frown. "What happened to you two?"

"Rain, rain and more rain," Ethan said, and forced James to step back when he swung his injured leg out of the car. He grabbed the crutch from the backseat, then shut the door. She watched James and Ethan head to the house.

She scrambled out, running after them with the key. "I forgot to give you this," she said to Ethan, but James took it from her.

"Thanks," he said, and she turned to head to her car.

After getting in, she watched Ethan and James go inside the house. Once the door was closed behind them, she realized that Ethan hadn't told her what he'd wanted to talk about.

She started her car. There was no way she'd go after him

and ask him; all she'd do was say something else embarrassing and make things worse. It always seemed to end that way with Ethan.

"It was nothing," she whispered as she drove back to town, away from Ethan. "Nothing." *That's a real lie,* she thought. There wasn't one thing about the man that amounted to nothing. He filled her every thought when he was around, and despite her best efforts, she was never unaware of his presence.

She arrived home and by the time she got inside, she felt exhausted. After taking a hot shower and dressing in an old college T-shirt for bed, she sat in the study and, to keep from going over and over the time she spent with Ethan, she did work to distract herself. She sorted through a stack of papers that her father hadn't gotten to. For as long as she could remember, her dad's desk had been piled with files he never got around to arranging.

But filing didn't help her stop a compulsive reliving of the past few hours. Finally, she left all of the papers where they were and went into the kitchen to make some tea. This was home, not just a house. The office was home, not just an old building. She knew that she wouldn't die if they lost it all, but she wasn't going to give up fighting for it. She couldn't. There weren't many options left, but one was available. One she didn't want to consider, but knew she had to.

She took her cup of tea back to the study to do some research, but as she passed the phone at the kitchen door, it rang. She quickly put the mug on a nearby table and answered. "Dr. Kelly."

Ethan didn't even bother identifying himself. "Sorry to bother you, Morgan."

She closed her eyes when he said her name, and knew that this time she had to say something that wasn't about them. "Ethan. I'm glad you called. I need to tell you something."

"Okay, what's that?"

She took a breath. "It's truly nothing personal, but I don't have any choices left. I'm going to see an attorney about fighting this whole mess, and I thought you should know."

ETHAN HAD BEEN restless since leaving Morgan, and when he finally lay down in bed, dressed in a fresh shirt and shorts, he'd remembered that he'd never asked her what he'd been wanting to in the car. It had been simple—an invitation to Joe's wedding party. He wanted her to come as his guest. But he'd never gotten the words out, not before she began apologizing for what had happened between them in the old house. Then, when she'd called it nothing, he could barely think of asking her.

Later, he knew that he wanted her at the party with him and he'd phoned to see if she'd take him up on the offer, hoping he could make her realize that what he felt wasn't nothing. It was something, and he wanted to figure it out. He knew a part of him had called just to hear her voice again, but when she spoke, he forgot how the softness in her tone made him feel alive. What she said, though, delivered a virtual blow to his middle. "You're going to do what?"

"You said yourself that, short of an injunction, there was no way to stop this development. And if I can stop it, then you won't have a reason to follow through on the lease business, and my father and I can either stay at least while the case goes through court, or we get to stay permanently." She spoke faster and faster as she went, as if building on her plan. "And maybe there's some sort of eminent domain statute that could apply, too."

He would have laughed at her if the whole idea hadn't been so horrendous. "Morgan, Morgan, stop. That isn't going to happen. Eminent domain doesn't apply. It's not your land we're trying to take for development, and it never was."

He heard her take quick, shallow breaths, but she didn't speak again.

"Are you still there?" he asked.

"Of course I'm here, and the eminent domain thing was just a thought. I don't know what an attorney will tell me, but I'm going to find out."

Ethan felt as if all the air had left his lungs, and he looked around the empty guest house as if he could find an answer somewhere in the shadowy corners. His leg throbbed, and even with it propped up on a pillow, it was annoying him. "It won't work. I told you, there are no zone violations, no conservation considerations, no ecological damage. There's no way to do what you're talking about doing."

"I want to hear that from an attorney."

He grimaced. "I'm not lying to you."

"Of course not," she said, but that statement came after just a second of hesitation. So much for her trusting him.

"And I'm just asking you to move, not walk the plank."

The tension between them was almost palpable. "Your roots are showing."

God, this was going downhill so fast it was making him dizzy. All he'd wanted to do was ask her to the party, and now she was giving him a pounding headache that was matching the throbbing in his leg. "Yeah, me and Bartholomew, out pillaging and plundering. You're lucky you got home in one piece tonight."

"This isn't personal," she said again, throwing his own words back at him. "Business is business. It's that simple for you, and it has to be that simple for me. No emotions."

If he wasn't incapacitated, he would have hung up and gone over to her place to do this face-to-face. But that thought stopped him dead. Face-to-face? No, if he was in the same room with her right then, he wouldn't be arguing with her. That's the last thing he'd want to do. The very last thing.

Chapter Eleven

"Yes, business is business," Ethan said through clenched teeth.

"I guess this is where I tell you that my attorney will be in touch with your attorney?" Morgan responded.

Ethan knew how lost he was dealing with Morgan when he did something he never remembered ever doing when faced with a business crisis. He surrendered. "Johanson."

"Excuse me."

"The attorney your attorney will need to contact is Chris Johanson in Seattle. I don't have his phone number on me, but you or your attorney can get it easily by contacting the office in the morning." He hesitated before adding, "And it's going to cost an arm and a leg to do anything."

"I know it won't be cheap, but I have to do it." She coughed softly, as if clearing her throat, then said, "And I will."

She was upset, he could hear it in her tone. Then he was giving her advice that he wished she'd take, as much for her sake as for his and the company's. "Sleep on it and really think about it before you do anything you might regret. Then do what you feel you need to do."

"Just do it?" she asked.

He flinched as more of his words were tossed back at him. "Yeah, just do it."

"It's getting late. I'll let you go."

"But I called you," he pointed out.

"Oh, right. What did you call for?"

He found himself closing his eyes as he realized he wasn't sure what to say now. After what she'd just told him, there wasn't a chance in hell she'd go to the wedding party as his guest. "Nothing important."

She paused, then said, "Okay, good night."

"Good night," he echoed, and the line went dead.

He'd lied to her. Emotions did come into his business dealings from time to time, and right then, frustration and anger all but choked him. He sat up, grabbed his crutch and headed out of the bedroom. He got as far as the door to the office, the cordless phone still clutched in his hand. He stared at it, then threw it with all his might against the couch near the hearth where Morgan had sat a few nights ago.

His resounding "Damn it all," mingled with the thump of the phone as it hit the leather cushions. It bounced, then tumbled onto the floor with a hard thud. Suddenly it rang. Morgan? Was she calling back? Had she changed her mind? He went as quickly as he could to where the phone lay and sank into the couch, then reached to pick it up.

By the time he hit the right button the ringing had stopped. He pushed his crutch away from him, letting it slip on the wooden floor to slide partway under the other sofa, and looked down at the LED readout on the handset. James had called. He called him back, and when the other man answered, Ethan snapped, "What did you want?"

"Whoa, who stepped on your chain?" Before Ethan could formulate an answer, James did it for him. "Oh, the good doctor?"

His friend was a mind reader. "Damn straight."

"I figured as much."

"How so?"

"You were gone for hours, came back and looking as if you'd stood under a shower fully dressed and the tension in the car when you got out was so thick you could've cut it with a knife. Call me stupid, but everything seemed to be directly related to the doctor."

"What did you call for?" Ethan asked abruptly, not about to explain what was going on with Morgan right now.

"Nothing," he said, and Ethan knew that James was getting annoyed. "Forget it."

He'd heard Morgan say "Nothing" tonight, and now James. He didn't believe either one of them. "Okay, I'm sorry. You're right. It's her. I just talked to her."

The man didn't gloat over the apology. "What happened?"

"She just told me that she's going to go to court to stop the Bartholomew Bay project."

"Man, she's really a feisty one, isn't she?"

"She's infuriating and annoying." He wouldn't go in to what else she was, not with James. "And she has a decent chance of dragging this out long enough to end the whole project."

"How can you stop her?"

He took a few moments to try to tamp down his lingering frustration before answering James. "I can't." He raked his fingers through his hair, then hit his thigh with the flat of his hand. "She's determined to do it. She sees losing that property as the end of everything she cares about."

"Did you ever wonder why it's so important to her?"

"She wants it. Her family has been there a long time, and she doesn't want to let it go. That or the idea of a four-bed clinic beside it. Problem is, they don't have the funds to do all they think they'd like to do, and they certainly don't have the funds for a prolonged legal fight." He remembered the Christmas decorations that almost made the aging building look inviting. "She looked at the properties on the list I put together, but none were suitable, mostly because they were nothing like the old place."

"Well, she struck me as a very intelligent woman, so she has to have pretty valid reasons to go through all of this in the hopes of hanging on to it."

"She said it's home. An office building—a pretty well outdated one at that—and the old house behind it. They're all irreplaceable to her? That's crazy. She's crazy."

"Why is the doctor driving *you* so crazy?"

Ethan almost dismissed that comment with a "Don't be crazy yourself," but he couldn't. Morgan *was* driving him crazy, and it had nothing to do with business. He kept trying to get close to her, only to be pushed away. He kept wanting to be with her and not think about the offices or the land. In fact, he just wanted to be with her.

MORGAN HAD FELT the real Ethan Grace had been tantalizingly close to the surface, especially when he'd held her in his arms and kissed her, but that man disappeared completely when business came into play. As she went about her rounds the next day, she couldn't get Ethan or the conversation she'd had that morning with her attorney, John Block, out of her mind.

"If you want me to do this, I'll look in to it," John had said over the phone. "But I have to warn you. You're like David tackling Goliath, and you don't even have a slingshot."

She'd told him to see what a lawsuit against the E.P.G. Corporation would entail, but her hopes had gradually faded to a sense of desperation when John told her, "The money will be a real issue. E.P.G. has unlimited funds, and they'll use them. They'll keep at it until you give up." He'd paused before adding, "I'm not telling you what to do, but you might want to think of another way to stop them besides taking them on in court."

She hadn't told him about her plan to get closer to Ethan, to get him to understand what was at stake in the hopes that he'd help her or maybe, ideally, cancel the whole project. That had been such a bust, it was painful to even think about now. "There isn't any other way of doing this," she'd told him.

"Okay," he'd said, then told her what it would cost for the preliminary workup.

She'd swallowed, but had given him the go-ahead to at least start. She'd figure out what to do after he looked in to the process and had a definitive figure for the costs. Then she'd gone in to work and faced an office full of colds and flu and people stressed out over the holidays.

Around noon she went into the same examination room where she'd fixed Ethan's cast the night before, and found a dark-haired seven-year-old girl who had a deep cough and a fever. Katie Owens was with her mother, Adella, a tiny dark woman who had gone to school with Morgan. "I'm so glad you could see us today," she said to Morgan.

Katie was on the exam table, playing with a rag doll and looking decidedly flushed. Morgan went right over to the child. "No problem, Adella, I'm just sorry Katie isn't feeling well."

"She's had a fever for a couple of days and a really deep cough at night. It's the fever that's bothering me most."

Morgan smiled at the little girl. "Okay, sweetie, I'm just going to check your chest." She put the stethoscope hanging around her neck into her ears and listened to Katie's chest. The congestion was apparent, but didn't sound as if it was in the lower lobes of the lungs. "Now your ears," she said and looked for infection.

She finally stood back and looked at the chart Sharon had left. "Her temperature isn't too elevated, but probably will go up at night." She smiled at the worried mother. "Don't ask me why that happens, it just does. And her congestion sounds worse than it is. Coughing is a natural way to get rid of that phlegm."

Adella moved closer to her daughter and hugged her to her chest. "Thanks, Morgan. I wasn't sure if you'd be up to doing all of this with what's going on."

"Excuse me?" she said, looking up from the notes she was making on the chart.

"With that Ethan Grace trying to take this place and put you all out."

"It isn't quite that simple," Morgan said as she wrote out a prescription for decongestant. "But I'm not going to let it go."

"I didn't think you would, but I don't understand how anyone could do this to you and your dad. Those Graces are real Grinches," she said. "Their hearts are two sizes too small."

Morgan knew Ethan had a heart—she'd felt it beat against her hand. She shook her head. "I'm not a cardiologist, so the heart isn't in my area of specialty, but I know that our hearts— mine and dad's—are here, and, if I can figure it out, we'll stay right here."

"Good for you, Morgan. We're behind you. If there's anything we can do, just ask. Maybe we can picket the company, or ask some human-interest reporter to do a story or have a fund-raiser? It can get expensive when lawyers are involved."

Morgan laid the chart down on the side cupboard and tried not to think of the money she was going to have to come up with in the near future. "Thanks, but for now, I talked to an attorney and he's going to look in to it. Until then, I think I just have to sit tight."

"Okay, but let us know if we can do anything or if you need anything." She helped her daughter put on her jacket. "We're here for you."

"Thank you. That means a lot."

"You bet," Adella said. "Is that all I need for Katie?"

Morgan handed her the prescription. "Give her this as soon as you can get it filled, and if the fever gets higher, call me."

"Thanks so much," Adella said and picked up Katie. "Call if you need help with the Graces."

"I will," Morgan assured her, then walked her out.

She motioned to Sharon to give her ten minutes before bringing in another patient, and she headed back to her father's office to take a break. She poured a cup of coffee and sat down behind her dad's desk. Sipping the hot liquid, she thought about how impossible it was for her to keep her emotions out of this whole business. She'd felt sick after getting off the phone with Ethan, and her stomach had been in knots thinking about what she was going to do ever since. But he had been so smooth, even giving her the name of his attorney and telling her to think on her decision.

She closed her eyes and exhaled a long breath, but it didn't ease her tense muscles. Everything was up in the air, her whole life on shaky ground, and Ethan was at the core of it. A man who could neatly block all emotions out of business, yet who had kissed her and touched her and made her think foolish things that came and went like lightning through the night. The man she thought she'd found had evaporated as soon as she'd mentioned the property.

He worried about what Darren had said, and she worried about the possibility that she was falling in love with a man who just might have a heart two sizes too small. That thought came and went in a blur. Falling in love with Ethan? She sat up straight, the coffee sloshing over the lip of the cup and splashing on her white coat.

She was attracted to Ethan, despite their differences, but in love with him? No, that wasn't possible. That was just plain insane. She'd never been close to being in love before, and had almost thought love was a rumor. But now, she wasn't sure what it was she was feeling.

"Morgan?"

She looked up at Sharon in the doorway. "What?"

The nurse came into the room. "Are you ready for the next patient? It's Apollo Walls." She grimaced. "He's sure he's got some sort of food poisoning and needs to talk to you about it."

"Okay," she said and stood to remove her jacket. She tossed it into an open hamper by the bookshelves and took a clean one from a stack on a file cabinet by her. "Tell him I'll be right there." She slipped on the fresh jacket, but didn't even think of buttoning it when she realized that her hands were shaking.

Sharon must have seen her unsteadiness. "You look pale. Are you getting sick? You've been seeing a straight run of cold and flu patients for the past week or more."

"No, I'm not sick."

"Then it's this office mess, isn't it?"

She couldn't refute that. Ethan was a huge part of the mess. "I'm not sure what's going to happen."

"I know. Life can get so confusing. But I'll always be here for you." Morgan was beyond confused at that moment. "I kind of thought, since you had been up to the Grace place and you were with Mr. Grace last night, that maybe you'd been able to—"

"How do you know that?" Morgan asked, thinking that the CIA had nothing on the gossip exchange on Shelter Island.

"Sylvia, my daughter's best friend, the daughter of—"

"I know Sylvia Short," she said.

"Well, then you know she works up at the Grace place— at least she will for the holidays and that big wedding reception—and she said you'd been up there with Mr. Grace and that the two of you went for a ride yesterday during the storm. Then Darren came by to replace the weather stripping on the front windows this morning, and he said he saw the two of you last night at the decrepit house across from the Paynes place on Hoover Street. He might have been confused."

"No, Darren wasn't," she said. "Mr. Grace was showing me some properties he thought we could move to."

"He thinks we could work in that building? It's so old it probably has gas lighting. I thought the man was supposed to be smart."

A bell sounded, and Sharon said, "Sorry, gotta check on the newcomers." She started to leave, but ducked her head back in. "Don't forget Walls in number two," she reminded, then hurried up front.

Morgan was pleasantly surprised to find out she could separate business from her personal life, at least for the short term. She took care of Apollo Walls, then the next patient and the next for the rest of the day and not once did she let herself think about Ethan. Around six when her last patient left, she went back to the office and sank down behind the desk. Sharon looked in on her. "I'm heading out. It's pretty foggy. They grounded the ferry, it's that bad. It made its last run, but couldn't head back to the mainland, so they berthed it at the dock here."

Heavy fog on the island was almost a given in the winter, but for it to get so bad the ferry couldn't make the second leg of its trip meant it was beyond bad. "Drive carefully," she said.

"Sure will."

Sharon returned to the waiting room, and the piped-in music stopped. Moments later, Morgan heard the front door open and close, leaving her alone.

Morgan sat back with a sigh, and there was no blocking

the thoughts she'd had earlier. She was quite sure she wasn't falling in love with Ethan, but she knew damn well that he affected her on a most basic level. Not that that would be a problem. She simply wouldn't be alone with him again, not after John filed the papers to start the lawsuit. If she saw him again, it would probably be in court anyway. No, not even then. She was positive that he wouldn't dirty his hands by being in court—he'd let his legal team do all the work.

She got up to take off her white jacket, but was startled when she heard someone banging on the front door. She went down the hallway, out into the waiting room. Through the glass window in the entry door, she saw a dark figure, then heard more banging. She squinted to try to make out who was there, but couldn't see anything beyond the dark silhouette. She couldn't even tell if it was a man or woman. "Who's there?" she called out.

"Sylvia Short."

Morgan unlocked the door and pulled it open. Sylvia was dressed all in dark clothes, bundled up against the cold. The fog was so heavy at her back that Morgan could barely see the lights from the store directly across from the office. "What's wrong?" she asked, when Sylvia made no move to come inside.

"Mr. Grace sent me to get you."

Morgan's heart lurched. "What?"

"It's Mr. Evans. He's unconscious and no one knows what's going on. We tried to call here but we got your service, and they said that they'd get a hold of you on your cell phone. Mr. Grace said not to wait and asked me to come down and bring you back to help poor Mr. Evans."

Morgan didn't ask any questions. She just hurried back into the office, grabbed her medical bag, her coat and her keys. She was back to Sylvia in less than a minute. "I'll drive and follow you," she said.

"Okay," the girl responded and rushed back to the big SUV that Morgan had driven the day before.

She got in her car, then headed north, keeping right behind Sylvia. Despite the emergency, their speed would have rivaled a snail's. The fog was everywhere, worse than Morgan could remember it being in a very long time. It was quite literally a wall in spots, and Sylvia slowed to inch her way through it. At one point, Morgan lost the taillights of the car in front of her, then they were there again, a vague red glow in the murky dark.

After what seemed an eternity, Sylvia turned to the right and they were at the estate. The gates stood open, and they drove up to the main house and to the side entrance. Morgan was out and running for the door before Sylvia had turned off her car. Morgan entered the house, then realized she didn't know where to go until she heard someone calling from the interior, "Sylvia? Is that you?"

The older woman Morgan had spoken to about Ethan's fall that first day saw Morgan and rushed to the door.

"Where do they want her?" Sylvia asked as she came up behind Morgan.

"In Mr. Evans's room."

Sylvia went around Morgan and said over her shoulder, "Follow me."

Morgan passed through the kitchen, then veered to the right, under an arch and to a set of steep stairs. Sylvia led the way up to the second level, then motioned to the left and down a long hallway that looked as if it had been chiseled out of stone. "This way."

Sylvia stopped at a door at the end of the hallway and stood aside to let Morgan enter a space that looked as if it was inside one of the turrets she'd seen from outside. The six-sided room was heavy with antique furnishings in rich burgundies and leather, and an enormous light fixture hung over a massive sleigh bed under a high-arched window.

She saw Ethan standing by the bed, and he didn't look away from James when he spoke to her. "He passed out an hour ago and hasn't come around." He stepped back to let her get a closer look. She quickly put her bag on the bed and started to examine him while she tossed questions over her shoulder. "Did he complain of anything out of the ordinary?"

"He had a hangover a few days ago and hasn't seemed himself since then, but—"

She cut off Ethan's explanation as she checked James's eyes, then listened to his heart and lungs. "Any headaches?"

"Yeah, he's had a bad one off and on. Bad enough that he came up to lie down a couple of hours ago."

"Throwing up?"

"No, but he said something about being nauseated."

"Difficulty breathing or swallowing?"

"No, but he hasn't been eating much. He said his vision was blurred, as if he couldn't focus."

She kept working while he spoke, but she had a hunch what was wrong. "Is there a history of diabetes or hypoglycemia in his family?"

"I don't know. He's never said much about his family."

She got some supplies out of the bag and laid them on the bed. Taking out a blood-sugar tester, she pushed James's forefinger into the cap and pressed the button. The man didn't flinch when the needle pierced his skin. She removed the tester, wiped his finger with a swab, then looked at the readout. The numbers were astronomical.

She stood back. "Who's his private doctor?"

"He's been to Dr. Perry a couple of times for flu shots, that sort of thing."

"You need to get that helicopter of yours to fly him to the

mainland, and I'll call your doctor to let him know that James is on his way so he can meet him at the hospital."

Ethan's face fell. "We can't fly anywhere. The fog's grounded all aircraft."

Morgan stood and tried to think what to do next. She'd never treated what she suspected was a diabetic coma, but she didn't have a choice. "Okay, get Dr. Perry on the phone. Maybe he can help me out, or find someone who can."

She'd barely stopped speaking when she heard Ethan already on the phone explaining what was going on to his physician. "Dr. Kelly's right here. She needs to talk to you."

She took the phone, found out he had some experience with diabetes, and that he could help as much as possible or call a specialist if necessary. She pushed that suggestion aside for now and told him about the blood sugar test and James's other symptoms. In a clear, concise manner, Dr. Perry questioned her. When he was done, he said that he concurred with Morgan's diagnosis of a diabetic coma and that she had no choice but to do what it took to help him.

She wrote down a list of supplies he told her to get. He said he would contact a specialist while she got things set up on her end, then hung up.

She turned to Ethan. "We think James is in a diabetic coma. He's probably had diabetes for a while, but was never diagnosed. The drinking might have triggered it, and…" She glanced at the side table and saw several candy wrappers. "He liked candy?"

"Not usually," Ethan said.

"It looks as if he ate quite a bit, and if he was already having blood sugar problems, the extra sugar could have pushed him over the edge." She picked up the list of supplies and called Sharon, who answered after only one ring. Without small talk, Morgan told her the situation, then gave her the list. Sharon knew Sylvia, so Morgan volunteered the girl for another trip in the fog. "Meet Sylvia at the office as quickly as you can."

"Do you need me to come up there?" she asked.

"No, I don't think so, just make sure you get everything I need on the list."

"I'll head to the office right now. Tell Sylvia to come in if I'm not waiting for her, and to go to the back."

Morgan hung up and turned back to Ethan. Before she could say anything, Sylvia stepped around him. "What do you need me to do?"

She explained, then the girl took off, and Ethan and Morgan were left together by James's bedside. She could see the worry on Ethan's face when he looked down at James, and she didn't hesitate to touch his hand. He never looked away from his friend as he laced his fingers with hers and held on to her. "How in the hell can a guy who's never been sick end up in a coma?"

"There's nothing predictable about human beings," she said and felt his fingers tighten on her hand.

"Are you sure about this being a diabetic coma?"

"No," she said honestly. "But I'm as certain as I can be without being able to run the tests I need. All I know is, with his symptoms and the blood sugar levels he has, it's the best bet."

He shifted and let her hand go to slip his arm around her shoulders. She felt his weight against her, and closed her eyes when he shuddered. "Then do what you need to do," he said in a rough voice.

She looked down at James, and knew that even though she and Ethan were going to be adversaries in the courtroom in the future, right now, they were on the same side. They were joined in some way, and she wrapped her arm around his waist and hugged him tightly. "I will," she said.

"I trust you."

He could trust her until the cows came home, but that wouldn't change anything if she was wrong. She pushed that thought aside, not willing to second-guess herself, not here, not now. She couldn't afford to.

"For all he does to annoy me, he's a good friend, a very good friend."

She looked up at Ethan, saw the tension etched in his face, and, acting on impulse, reached to touch his cheek with her free hand. "I know," she said softly and realized that the idea of loving this man wasn't all that impossible. Part of her wondered if she'd already fallen for him.

He shook his head, then let her go and, without using his crutch, awkwardly made his way back to the chair. Sinking into it, he sat forward and dropped his head into his hands. Morgan had to turn away from him to make herself focus on James and not on Ethan's pain. She prepared as much as possible, then all she could do was wait for Sylvia's return.

Ethan didn't move until a chime sounded in the room, then he looked up. "She's back."

"Stay with James," Morgan said as she left the room and headed back the way she'd come. She met Sylvia at the door and took one of the canvas bags she was carrying, along with a wooden box. Then she hurried back up the stairs to James's room. She rushed inside, moved pictures and paperwork off the massive dresser near the bed, then laid out her things. She glanced over at Ethan. "Go and get some rest. I've got what I need and it's going to take time for me to finish."

His dark eyes met her gaze. "No, I'm not leaving."

Morgan always tried to get relatives and loved ones out of the treatment room before she did anything for the patient— she couldn't afford distractions. Ethan was worse than that. She was aware of his every move, his every breath. There was no way she could fully concentrate with him there. "Please go. I promise I'll take care of him."

He looked at the bed, then back at her. He must have read it in her face how much she really needed him to go. He pushed himself to his feet and reached for his crutch. "Let me know, no matter what?"

"Of course."

"I'll be in my old room down the hall," Ethan said, and when he left, she reached for the phone. She put in a call to Dr. Perry, who answered immediately. "I've got everything you suggested. Can you stay on the phone with me for a while?"

"Absolutely."

Morgan took a deep breath, then said, "Okay, what's the best way to start?"

Chapter Twelve

Ethan made his way back to the turret room for the third time around four o'clock in the morning. The fog continued to keep everything at a standstill, but the helicopter was set to take off as soon as they had clearance in Seattle. He'd gone back to see James twice, and each time, Morgan had been intent on what she was doing, barely glancing at him. Ethan didn't understand what she was doing, but she kept saying, "It'll take time. It'll take time."

He wondered if James, who was still comatose, had any more time? He never moved. Morgan poked and prodded him, shifting him in the bed, but there was no response. Ethan had left the last time when he'd heard Morgan whispering to James as she leaned over him, checking his eyes with her light. "Hang in there. Just hang in there."

He didn't miss the unsteadiness in her voice, and he hadn't been able to stay in the room. But an hour later, he was back again. He paused as he reached the open door and braced himself when he heard nothing but silence inside. When he finally stepped into the room, he didn't see Morgan anywhere. Then he went toward the bed and spotted her curled up in the nearby high-backed chair.

She was sleeping sideways, her back against one arm, her

legs over the other. Her eyes were closed, and he simply looked at her for a long moment. God, she was lovely, despite the paleness from lack of rest and makeup on her face.

He turned to James, who looked peaceful, with decent color to his skin. The IV Morgan had Sylvia bring from her office was in the man's left arm, with two bags hanging from the hooks. He saw the rise and fall of the blanket draped over James's chest with each breath he took, then turned back to Morgan.

Her lashes lay in dark arcs on her cheeks, and her lips were softly parted. She made a low sigh, then shifted, her eyes fluttering open. She suddenly scrambled to sit up.

"What?" she asked, looking up at Ethan, then getting to her feet. "Oh, God, I fell asleep," she said, going to the bed. She seemed as alert as if she'd never dozed. She quickly checked James, then stood back with a deep exhalation of air. "Thank goodness," she breathed. "He's sleeping."

"He's been sleeping," he pointed out.

"No," she said, giving Ethan a shaky smile. "He's *sleeping,* I mean really sleeping. Normally."

He shook his head. "Are you sure?"

"Ethan," she said, her smile growing. "I think he's going to be okay."

That was all he needed to hear. He caught her to him, wanting to touch her. He held her against him, his face buried in her hair, and she embraced him. "Thank God," he whispered. "Thank God it's over."

She rubbed her forehead against his chest. "It's not over, but it's so much better," she said, her voice muffled against his shirt.

She pulled back from him, and he hated it when she let go of him to fumble in her pocket to take out her phone. "I promised Dr. Perry I'd call."

Ethan moved away from her as she made the call and only

vaguely listened to her conversation. He stood over James, watching him, so relieved. If he'd ever been given to tears, he would have cried.

Then Morgan was beside him, the phone put away, and she bent to brush James's forehead. "He still needs to get back to the mainland to have further tests, and to make sure everything is as good as it looks."

Then, as if it was the most natural thing in the world to do, she put her arm around his waist. He pulled her closer and whispered, "You're terrific."

James moaned, and they turned to him. The next instant his eyes fluttered open. James was back. He squinted, looking from Ethan to Morgan, and licked his lips. "What are…?" He looked confused. "You two…you…you look as if you're going to a funeral."

Ethan shook his head. "You are so wrong this time," he said.

"Then…what's wrong?"

Morgan let go of Ethan to bend over James, and while she checked his vitals, Ethan stayed right behind her. She pricked his finger to check his blood levels, and James flinched. "Ouch," he said, then Morgan stood and looked at a small meter she had in her hand.

"Much, much better," she said. "You're going to be fine." She stroked his forehead and kept talking. "You had us scared for a while."

"Why?"

"Do you have any history of diabetes?"

He looked really confused now. "Me? No. My mother, she was diabetic, but not me." He frowned. "What is this all about?" he asked, and moved as if to get up. Morgan quickly put her hands on his shoulders and eased him back into the pillows.

"Just take it easy. You need to stay still and rest. Ethan called me because you were unconscious, and he couldn't wake you up. It looks if you were in a diabetic coma, but that's over and you're going to be fine. They'll fly you to the mainland as soon as the fog lifts, and Dr. Perry will check you out and make sure you're stabilized."

James still looked confused. Tired, he simply said, "Whatever you say," and closed his eyes.

Mrs. Forbes came in, clearly sleepy after being up much of the night. "Sir, I came to—"

"Call Scooter at the hangar and tell him we need him as soon as possible."

"That's what I was coming to tell you. He's on his way and will be here in less than five minutes." As if on cue, he heard the chop-chop sound of the propeller.

"Great, tell him to get up here as quickly as he can."

She hurried off, and Ethan turned to find Morgan talking to James. "We were so lucky," she whispered, almost to herself. "So very lucky."

Ethan watched her hand touch James's cheek, then press her fingers to the pulse at his throat. James opened his eyes a slit. "Are you through?"

She drew back with a faint chuckle. "I am, but it's just starting for you. The helicopter is here."

"I heard," he mumbled a bit thickly. "I hate flying."

"You'll love this," Ethan said. "Scooter piloting."

"Oh, no," he groaned and closed his eyes. "Not Scooter."

"Oh, yes, Scooter," a voice said from behind them, and Ethan turned to find the pilot. Al Scooter was short and stocky, with a totally bald head and a mustache so thick it looked like a whisk broom. "And I hear you're all messed up," he said to James as he came closer. Two other men wearing EMT uniforms were with him carrying a stretcher. "Do we pick you up, or are you going to get on that thing yourself?" Scooter asked as he motioned to the stretcher.

James pushed himself up, grimacing when he did it, then one of the other men quickly got to him. The second man unhooked the IV and looped it into an extension on the gurney. In less than a minute, James was being covered with a blanket and strapped down. He looked at Ethan. "I'll get you for this, boss," he said.

"I'll look forward to it," Ethan said, then waved to Scooter. "Take good care of him."

"That's the plan," he said, and Ethan and Morgan followed the crew back down the hallway to an elevator that had been put in for the service staff. The stretcher took up most of the space, so Morgan and Ethan stayed behind to let the others go down. By the time the elevator came back for Ethan and Morgan, the team was almost to the helicopter that had landed between the main house and the guest house.

Morgan supervised James as he was placed on the helicopter, then let the EMTs take over. Scooter gave Ethan a thumbs-up sign as the helicopter's motor revved up, then they lifted off.

Ethan could sense the relief in Morgan to have James on his way, and it was echoed in him. He'd barely been able to breathe while the outcome of the man's health had been uncertain. He ran a hand over his face, watched the helicopter disappear into the fog that still hung low over the water, then exhaled harshly. "Thank goodness they were able to get here," he whispered.

Morgan was so close he felt her arm brush his when she shifted. "He'll be fine. Dr. Perry is meeting them at the landing pad, and he'll supervise his care."

Ethan looked down at Morgan, at her hands clenched in front of her and thought, *The hands really show her feelings. She's scared, despite her reassuring words.* She seemed achingly vulnerable at that moment. The woman had probably saved James's life, and she was still terrified.

Wanting to shoulder her fears, he pulled her to his side, loving her heat against him in a cold world. "You bet he'll be fine. He had a great doctor."

She looked up at him, her eyes overly bright, and he wondered if she was going to break down. Doctors dealt with life and death all the time, and it was unnerving to him to see her so tangled up in James's survival. "I did the best I could," she murmured as the sounds of the helicopter finally died out in the small hours of the morning.

"I know, I know," he said, and tangled his fingers in her hair to press her head to his chest. "I know."

"Oh, damn," she mumbled against his shirt. "Damn."

"What?"

She moved back, but not far enough so he had to let go of her. She held up her hand and it was shaking uncontrollably. "Nerves. It always happens. I…I guess it's the relief."

"That's natural," he said.

She licked her lips, then turned, breaking the contact with him. "I need to call Dr. Perry to let him know James is safely on his way," she said, as a jarring sensation of being stranded washed over him. He kept his hands at his sides and watched her make her call. She shut the phone abruptly. "Damn it, it's dead. I'll use the phone in the house."

Just as she turned to leave, he stopped her. "No, use the phone in the guest house. It's right there."

She nodded and, without a word, headed to the guest house. He followed more slowly on the crutch, and by the time he got inside, Morgan was already on the phone in the living area, listening intently. Finally she spoke. "Yes, yes, that's it. Please let me know. My cell phone is dead, so call me here at Ethan's. Thank you for everything."

She hung up, but put in another call right away. "It's me," she said. "My cell phone's dead. You can reach me at this number for now." She read the number off the receiver. "I'll call when that changes."

Ethan moved over to her and when she hung up, he was inches from her. She looked delicate and so very tired. Feelings he couldn't remember ever having for a woman came full force. She'd just saved a life, and he wanted to save her. He wanted to wipe the weariness from her expression, to hold her and tell her how proud he was of her. He wanted to touch her, to feel her against him and to love her.

He felt his breath catch in his chest at the thought. He stared down at her, at her shadowed smudged eyes, her softly parted lips, and he knew that he wanted her. It was that simple and that complicated. He turned away from her, not sure he could be close her and be so unselfish as to say, "Take my bed and rest."

But as he moved, he didn't realize the table was so close to his crutch. He felt a jerk when it caught the table leg. Morgan caught the phone in midair, but the table wasn't so lucky. It teetered, then fell with a crack on his cast. The blow robbed him of his balance, and he went down. A second later he was on his back on the floor, and Morgan was leaning over him.

"Are you okay?"

He looked up at her and realized that their first meeting, when he'd opened his eyes to find her standing over him, had led to this moment and he knew without a doubt that, despite all the detours, arguments and problems, he was falling in love with this woman.

She pressed her hand to his forehead, her fingers moving to his throat to feel his pulse. His heart had to hammering. "I'll get you up," she said. "Just help if you can."

With that, her hand caught one of his, and he reached with the other to grab the back of the sofa. Together, they got him to his feet, then Morgan pulled his arm around her shoulders. "Come on," she said, and he let her help him to the bedroom.

She intended to get him on the bed, but he didn't let go of her as he fell into the linens. Surprised, she tumbled with him. By the time Morgan righted herself, she was on top of him once again, and he knew that he wasn't going to let her go. Not yet.

MORGAN COULDN'T think straight. Relief and nervousness had consumed her in equal measure after James woke up, and now she was with Ethan in his bed. Straddling him, she knew she should push off him and just leave, but she didn't—she couldn't. There was no strength left in her for anything, least of all for a fight against what she felt for this man. She was tired from the long night she'd had with James, tired of worrying about the offices and the land and tired of pretending that Ethan meant nothing to her. The enemy? Not even close, she conceded as he caressed her face, his fingertip tracing her lips.

She hardly knew him, but she felt as if she'd known him all her life. The real Ethan. The man lying so close to her. The man with eyes as dark as night and a heat that seemed to filter into her soul. His hand brushed at her hair, skimming over her skin, then gently cupped the back of her neck to ease her even closer to him. "Stay," was all he said in a low voice.

She didn't move because she was quite certain if she did, she'd fly into a million pieces from the frantic need that filled her for this man. If she let herself touch him, kiss him and let him make love with her, she knew she'd never be the same. She was afraid that once she started, there would be no turning back. Yet she knew that didn't matter. She would never be the same after she was with him, but she needed Ethan in her life.

She hesitantly touched her lips to his and tasted him. He

opened to her, letting her tentatively run her tongue over his teeth, before entering him. Emotions overwhelmed her. She looked down at him, taking in every shape and angle of his face, then touched the buttons on his shirt. She tried to undo the fasteners, but her hands were so incredibly shaky that she couldn't manage even one.

Ethan helped her, one button, two buttons, then muttering in frustration, he simply ripped open his shirt. She touched his sleek chest, running her fingers over him, feeling his muscles and the heat radiating from his skin. She circled one nipple with her fingertip and thrilled when he arched at the contact, his eyes closing, pressing his arousal against her. He wanted her as much as she wanted him, and if she had had any patience to go slowly, to explore him and find out everything about him, it was now gone.

He reached for her, pulled her down, meeting her mouth with his. He ravaged her with his kiss, building a fire in her that threatened to consume her. His hands pulled at her sweater, tugging it up, and throwing it onto the floor. Her bra followed, and Ethan cupped her breasts, then his lips found her nipple. She gasped at the intensity of the pleasure that tugged deep inside her, and she shifted over and off him, scrambled off the bed and, without taking her eyes off of Ethan, stripped out of her boots and jeans.

His dark gaze was unblinking when she came closer and he hooked his forefinger into the band of her panties. He eased the skimpy covering down, and she wasn't embarrassed as she took them off and stood before him. She wanted him. She wanted to know everything about him, every part of him, to hear every breath he took. And she didn't want any barriers at all.

His eyes skimmed over her, then he met her gaze and said, "Come here."

She did as he said, but didn't get back in bed with him. She stood over him, bending to help him slip off his shirt. She ran her hand over his chest, down to his taut stomach, then lower to the fastener for his shorts, which barely contained him now. His hand covered hers, easing her touch lower until she felt his hardness.

She heard his sharp intake of air, and she pulled at the snap and the zipper. He awkwardly lifted his hips, letting her strip him naked. Before she could do more than see him and feel a surge of more desire flare in her, he pulled her onto the bed with him, tangling them in the sheets. She felt her knee strike his cast, but if there was pain, it didn't seem to register. Being close to him was everything. Skin against skin. Nothing between them. Just the two of them.

He kissed her, his hands on her, and any thought of a gentle coming together disappeared. His ragged breathing echoed her own, and she couldn't get enough of his taste or his touch. There was a freedom in her that she'd never known could exist with a man. But it was there and growing. She straddled him, kissing his chest, his stomach, then she found him.

His gasp filled the room, followed by a low groan as she kissed him and felt his hardness. Before she could go further, he reached for her hands, easing her back up, and she felt him tremble. His eyes glowed in the darkness, and his voice was hoarse. "Damn it, this cast," he muttered through clenched teeth. "I want you. I want to be in you," he rasped.

Since he couldn't bring himself to her, she went to him, bracing herself with her hands by his shoulders, and feeling him against her. His hand went down between them, guiding himself slowly into her. She closed her eyes tightly, feeling every inch of him as he slipped deeper and deeper inside her. When he'd filled her, Morgan held her breath, almost afraid to move in case the sensations that ran riot through her grew stronger. She wasn't sure if she could endure that much pleasure at one time.

His hands moved to her hips, lifting her, then lowering her, and as he thrust into her, she knew she wanted everything from him. She wanted to know him as she'd never known another man. She met thrust for thrust. Her arms were shaking and her breathing came in ragged gasps as the sensations grew and grew.

She arched back and heard soft moans that she knew were hers. They mingled with Ethan's. "Yes, yes, yes," she said, as he pushed higher and higher. Just when she thought she couldn't go any higher, she flew to a place where her body seemed to melt into his, and she understood what it meant to be one with another human being.

Then softly, ever so gently, she began to tumble back to reality with him. Letting herself lie on him, she held him, breathed with him, and heard his heart pounding against her cheek. His fingers were tangled in her hair, and she kissed his sleek, damp skin. The saltiness only added to the reality that came slowly out of the haze of scattering feelings. She loved him. She simply loved him.

She closed her eyes, letting the thought settle in her, and she embraced it the way she did the man beneath her. She kissed his chest again, then carefully eased to the side, hating to leave him, but never letting go of him, either. His arm held her to his side, and she felt him press a kiss to the top of her head. She rested her hand over his heart and shifted to rest her leg over his. Closing her eyes, she just let herself feel. His skin, his breath on her, his hand on her hip, her breasts against his side. Feel. Feel. And remember. She began to drift, and just before she let sleep come, she thought she heard Ethan whisper, "Thank you."

ETHAN LAY in the shadows, holding Morgan next to him as he felt her fall asleep, and he stared up at the ceiling. He'd thought he might love her. That he wanted her with him. That he wanted to make love with her, at least once. But as they'd made love, he'd known he'd been wrong. It wasn't that he might love her. He did, but he wanted so much more. He needed her for as long as he drew breath. He closed his eyes, and pressed his lips to her hair.

This was all new to him, and he wasn't quite sure what to do. He thought of asking her to stay and leave it at that, but before he could get anything straight in his own mind, he simply whispered, "Thank you," and held her against him.

The next instant the phone rang, waking Morgan.

She sat up and pushed back her hair. "I've got it," she said, reaching over him to grab the phone.

Her naked breasts skimmed over his chest, and his body tightened. "Dr. Kelly." Then, "Yes, Dr. Perry."

Ethan watched her as she listened to the doctor on the other end. He tensed when a frown tugged a line between her blue eyes, but then she sank back in the pillows and breathed, "Wonderful, just wonderful." She swiped at her face, and he realized she was crying. "I don't know what would have happened—" She gulped, then said softly, "Thank you. Yes, please, let me know."

She sat back as she lowered the phone into the tangle of sheets on her legs. "What?" Ethan asked.

"It *was* insulin shock, and James is going to be fine. They have his blood sugar under control, and Dr. Perry doesn't think there'll be any complications if he follows instructions."

Ethan took the phone from her limp grip, put it back on the nightstand, then turned to Morgan. He covered her hand with his, and pulled her down to him. "Come here," he said, reveling in the feel of her naked, swollen breasts against his chest. He brushed her hair back when it fell forward to veil her face partially, and he smiled at her. "You're terrific."

"I was lucky," she said. "I didn't have what I needed, and I made wild guesses. I was so worried—"

His fingers tangled in her hair and he drew her down to him when she started to sob. He let her cry, holding her, thankful that James was okay, and so thankful that she was here with him. When she quieted, she shifted, then raised herself on her elbow to look down at him. He touched her damp cheeks, brushing them with his thumb. "You *are* so terrific," he said, and he didn't just mean as a doctor.

She took a shaky breath, then kissed him, the taste of tears on her lips and his body was responding again. She drew back, her hand pressed to his chest. "So are you," she whispered.

He wanted to say that he'd never known anyone like her, or had never felt this way about anyone, but the words stopped when she gave him a deep and searching kiss as if she couldn't get enough of him. He knew he couldn't get enough of her, and no matter how sated he thought he'd been before, he wanted her again and again and again. The cast restricted what he could do, but it didn't stop Morgan.

She moved to the right a bit, freeing her left hand, which she laid on his stomach, then slid lower and lower, finding him. He instinctively arched upward. He ached for her, and he cupped her breasts, feeling her response as her nipples hardened. Then his hand followed the path hers had taken, and he found her moist heat. She trembled at the contact. "Oh, yes," she breathed, when he slipped a finger into her. "Yes." The single word echoed over and over again and again as he moved in her.

She kissed him with a breathtaking fierceness, then caught his hand, urging him to do more. He slipped into her with ease, a perfect fit as if they were made for each other. He shifted, moving farther into her, then caught her by the waist, helping her raise and lower herself. There was no gradual buildup, no slow-and-easy coming together. He wanted her and he had her. Feelings soared in him, and she seemed to be everywhere. He felt as if he was melding into her in some stunning way that he couldn't begin to fathom.

They went higher and higher, faster and faster, and when he thought he couldn't stand it anymore, they climaxed together. Their cries mingled together, and she was holding to him, coming down with him, never letting him leave her.

They lay like that for what seemed an eternity before Morgan snuggled into him with a deep sigh that matched his own. The world was absolutely right at that moment, and he didn't want it to change. He had found a spot where he was happy. Period. And he wanted it to last forever.

Chapter Thirteen

Morgan woke with a start and found she was alone in Ethan's bed. Everything about last night came to her in a rush and the memory almost took her breath away. She sat up and looked around the room. The clock showed seven-fifteen, and remarkably, there was sunlight coming through the windows that faced the water. It wasn't warm and fuzzy sunlight, but cold and thin, no fog or rain was present.

She glanced at the closed door, then back to the bed and the pillow that still held the impression of Ethan's head. She felt anxious, needing to see him, and feeling empty with him gone. She'd never dreamed this would happen. She'd never dreamed that she would have wanted Ethan as much as she had and did. She wasn't sure what they would do now, but she knew that she'd finally found the real Ethan—the caring, loving Ethan—and it gave her hope for their future.

A knock sounded on the door, and she reached for the rumpled sheet to cover her nakedness. As much as she wanted him to be next to her, she felt oddly vulnerable, and she crushed the sheet in her grip. "Yes?"

It wasn't Ethan who walked into the room but Mrs. Forbes. She didn't bat an eyelash at seeing Morgan in Ethan's bed.

"Dr. Kelly, I spoke to Dr. Perry and he said that you did a terrific job helping our James."

Morgan knew she was blushing, partly from being naked in the man's bed and partly from the flattery that was being relayed to her. "I'm just glad James is going to be okay."

Mrs. Forbes came a bit closer, and Morgan could see she had something clutched in her hand. "We—the whole staff— want to thank you for what you did, too. James is very important to all of us, especially to Mr. Grace." She stopped and looked down at her hand. "Oh, I almost forgot. Mr. Grace had this charged for you last night. Your phone is like Sylvia's, and she had her charger…" She shrugged, then laid the cell phone on the side table. "Thank you again for all you did for James."

Morgan nodded, then the lady left, closing the door behind her. Morgan let go of her death grip on the sheet and stretched across the bed to grab her phone. She turned it on, saw that she had two messages, and called her voice mail. The first was from Sharon telling her to call her as soon as she could. She was worried and wanted to make sure everyone was okay. The second one was from her father.

"It's me, Dad, just checking in, letting you know that I'm having a good time. I just wish I was going to be with you at Christmas, but I'll see you right after New Year's and we'll have a long talk. Merry Christmas. I love you."

Morgan erased the message, then called Sharon. When the woman answered on the second ring, Morgan said, "It's me."

"What's going on there? They said the helicopter came early this morning and took Mr. Evans to the mainland. Then you weren't answering your phone, and I thought you might have gone with him."

She had no doubt that Sylvia had filled Sharon in on just about everything. She just hoped that her being in Ethan's bed hadn't been part of the briefing. "No, I didn't. James was in insulin shock, and I managed to stabilize him, then they took him to Seattle. I'm still at the Grace estate." She closed her eyes. "I might be a bit late getting to the office. It's been a long night."

"Try to get some rest, and I'll cover for you. I can diagnose a cold with the best of them."

"No playing doctor. Just cancel the morning appointments and move the most pressing to the afternoon schedule. I'll stay as long as I have to tonight."

"Sure thing," Sharon said and hung up.

Morgan sank back into the pillows, staring up at the ceiling. She loved Ethan. It was that simple and that complicated. He'd never said anything about love during the night, and she'd kept her feelings to herself. Now she needed to tell him—to figure out what her next step should be. She got out of bed, found her clothes and put them on. Combing her hair as best she could with her fingers, she pushed her feet into her boots, then headed to the door.

She stepped out into the living area, didn't see anyone, but heard Ethan speaking in the office. His voice was too low for her to make out what he was saying until she was almost to the open door.

"There isn't anything else to discuss. The reality is, the business is dying, and you don't have enough sense to jump ship before you go down with it. That's the chance I'm giving you. A lifeboat."

She stopped dead when another man spoke up, and she realized Ethan wasn't on the phone, but actually meeting with someone in his office. "It's a family business," the man almost pleaded. "We've had it for twenty years. Selling it off to you so you can chop and dice it… I can't let that happen. I won't let it happen."

She went a step closer and saw Ethan sitting behind his desk, his cast resting on a low stool; she saw only the other man's back. He was in a dark overcoat and she didn't miss his hands, which were clenched in tight fists at his sides.

"You don't have a choice," Ethan said. He didn't seem concerned with what the other man was saying. "Either we take the company, or it collapses. You don't have the skill or money to fix it. You have to accept that and move on. It's just a business."

Morgan swallowed hard at his words. *It's just a business.*

"How do you move on when you see what you've loved falling apart around you? That you're losing all you've worked for in your life. It's just human to try to hold on."

"Now that's your mistake—letting emotions get involved. If you do that, you'll never get anywhere."

There was heavy silence while Ethan looked steadily at the man. "I thought if I talked to you away from the office, one on one, that you'd understand."

Ethan never blinked. "I understand and I'm telling you that you'd be a fool to hang on to a sinking ship. We're going ahead with the takeover. It's in the works and it won't be stopped."

The man threw his hands up as if motioning to everything around him. "This is a perfect setting for you. You're worse than a pirate. At least with a pirate, the swords leveled the playing field a bit. I don't have any defense against a man like you." He was shaking now, but Ethan hadn't moved. "Damn you."

With that, the man spun around and headed for the door, opening it so quickly Morgan barely had time to get out of his way before he would have run into her. He didn't give her a glance, but Morgan saw such desperation and pain in his face that it tore at her. "Sorry," he muttered and kept going. He slammed the front door behind him.

Morgan turned and saw Ethan was still in his chair, except now he was watching her. She thought she'd found the real Ethan last night, but this was an Ethan she couldn't stand to be near.

"Regan Daniels," he said. "He runs Long and Daniels Shipping and Freight. At least, he did."

Ethan had dressed in a fresh white shirt, along with khaki shorts. Her stomach twisted and she almost thought she could taste him on her lips and feel him against her. "Why did he come here at this time in the morning?"

"His business is going under, and we're acquiring it. He came to convince me to back off. But he doesn't have a choice—it's a done deal." He paused, then said, "But I don't want to talk about business." He motioned her to come to him. "I want to talk about you and me." He smiled and his face transformed into the face of the man she loved.

She went to him and crouched, holding on to the arm of the chair. "Ethan, can't you help him?"

His smile was gone as quickly as it had come. He touched her face, running his finger along her jaw, then her lips. "I said no business. Not here."

She reached to take his hand in hers. "But it's his business and it sounds like it's his life. Can't you help him and get it back on its feet?"

"I'm not a doctor, Morgan. That's your department. I don't heal people. I'm a businessman."

"And never the twain shall meet?"

He bent toward her, and whispered, "Oh, I want the twain to meet, as long as it's you and me."

She didn't laugh. She stood and clasped her hands in front of her. She wouldn't let him see how disappointed she was right then, even though she felt as if she was about to break. "What about Daniels?"

He tipped back in the chair to look up at her. "Morgan, I'm not in the business of rescuing people."

Her heart sank more and more with each word, and she wondered if she'd imagined the man he'd been last night. She had to ask one thing. "Is that how you see my dad's office and the land by it? That we have poor business skills and we need you to fix things?"

"Oh, come on—" he started to say, but she cut him off.

"You're not rescuing us. We didn't make any mistakes. We help the islanders, people like James. Can't you see that we're needed here, that we can't just take a break and somewhere down the road relocate? That view doesn't save lives, good medical care does. And if we had the land next door, we could gradually put together a really wonderful clinic, and I'd have the testing facilities that I needed so desperately for James and didn't have."

Ethan studied her, his eyes narrowing as she bit her lip to stop saying more. "You saved James's life and you did it all out of your little black bag," he said in an even voice that was in direct contrast to the way her way her voice had risen emotionally. "And I've told you over and over again that there has to be another location you could use. You're just nostalgically connected to the old offices, and you're letting that put you offtrack. You need to face the truth and try to make your business efficient and stable wherever it is."

She felt as if she was fracturing into a million pieces. She'd been so blind. She'd been a fool. She'd let herself fall in love with this man, who she realized was nothing more than a stranger. Emotions hadn't served her well at all. "I am facing the truth," she managed to get out in a tight voice.

"What truth?"

"The truth that I let my feelings make me believe that you had a heart. I thought I felt it last night, but now I know I never did." She was crying and didn't care. She let the tears trail down her cheeks without making any effort to wipe them away. "What I can't figure out is, how you can live with yourself with all the destruction you leave in your wake. You don't care about anything, and you know—" she gulped to be able to finish "—I feel sorry for you."

Why had she thought that just because she loved him, that he would see what he was doing was wrong? She must have imagined the gentleness in him because she'd wanted it so much. She must have imagined that James's emergency would make him reconsider going ahead with the deal.

"Don't waste your time feeling sorry for me," he said tightly and Ethan Grace the businessman was back full force.

She had to ask one last time, even though she knew what he'd say. "Is there *any* way I can get you to let my father keep his home and office?"

His dark eyes, which had grown colder and colder, studied her intently. "Business is business."

She went numb. It was amazing to be in so much pain one minute, then feel next to nothing. She looked right at him. "It's nothing personal. And I bet old Bartholomew didn't make his conquests personal, either. Do what he did, Ethan— wrap yourself in your bounty, and maybe have a festival to celebrate your victories."

"You and I—" he started to say, but when he moved as if to touch her again, she jerked back quickly. She was terrified that if she let him near her the numbness would dissolve, and she knew she couldn't survive what she'd feel then.

"You and I have nothing," she said. He didn't speak or move, and she found herself talking just to fill the silence. "I just hope that you live the way Bartholomew did, alone on the cliffs, sur- rounded by his treasures, with no one to mourn your passing."

The numbness was a total blessing right then. She could

take in the set of his mouth, his sleep-rumpled hair, even the
sleek strength of his chest where the shirt parted, and not
dissolve into tears for what might have been. She'd forget this
moment eventually, but she knew she'd never stop loving the
man she'd found for such a short time, for a very long time.
She just hoped it wasn't forever.

"What about the lawsuit?"

If she'd been feeling anything, she knew his question would
have destroyed her. With their relationship falling apart, all he
cared abut was if he'd be sued or not. But she was able to look
right at him, and say, "You won't reconsider the development?"

"No."

She had her answer. She didn't want to be anywhere
around this man when her feelings returned, and she knew the
pain would come back sooner or later. When it did, she hoped
she'd survive it.

She walked out of the room and headed blindly to the
door. She was stunned when Ethan grabbed her by her arm
and jerked her to a stop. She pulled against him, but he held
her tightly, and she finally had to turn to face him again.
"Don't go like this," he implored.

She met his black eyes and wondered why life had to be
so perverse? Why had she ever met him? Why had she ever
thought she knew him? Why had she made love with him?
More importantly, why had she fallen in love with him?
"I…have to get to the office. Patients are waiting."

"Are we going to see each other in court?" His hold on her
was hovering just this side of real pain.

She knew she'd never go to court against him—she never
wanted to see him again. "No. We'll find another place for
the clinic. We'll see patients wherever we can, and live somewhere else. You can have the view and the land. Tear down

everything. My emotions aren't tied up in brick and mortar. It's not the building, it's what it represents."

"Just like that, the lawsuit ceases to exist?"

"Just like that," she muttered, as quickly and as irrevocably as her hopes. She stopped struggling to free herself, not having the strength to fight on any level. "You'll have time to pillage and plunder to your heart's content, and I'll go back to my life and try to pick up the pieces."

Without warning, he pulled her to him and kissed her with harsh fierceness before releasing his grip. "Go and do what you have to do."

She spun away from him and ran out of the house. She was almost to the main house when she realized she'd left her cell phone on the bedside table. She stopped, but didn't go back. There was no way she could do that. She looked up when Mrs. Forbes called to her from the side door. "Dr. Kelly? Are you all right?"

Morgan jogged toward the woman, trying to get control of her breathing. "I have an emergency," she gasped, and hurried past the woman into the house. "Please, could you get my cell phone from the guest house? I left without it," she called over her shoulder as she reached the stairs.

She rushed up to the turret room, got her black bag and set the rest of the supplies on the dresser. By the time she headed down with her bag, Mrs. Forbes was there with the cell phone. "Is there something wrong?" she asked.

Morgan took the phone without breaking her stride. "Ask Mr. Grace," she said. "Please, could you have the supplies I left in Mr. Evans's room sent to my office when you can?"

"Of course."

She left the Grace estate and felt as if she was driving away from any hope she'd had. In the blink of an eye, it was all gone and she was alone. Her vision started to blur and she had to pull off the road. She parked, put her hands over her eyes and the numbness evaporated in a painful rush, leaving her shaking and in tears.

THE HELICOPTER set down on the lawn between the main house and the guest unit, and Ethan got out, thankful to have the old, heavy cast gone. He'd been fitted for what the doctor called, a "minimum support walker." His fracture was healing well, and Ethan had decided he could function just fine in the city. He'd leave the island after Joe's wedding the next day and get back to his real life. His stay on the island was feeling more and more like being a "time out of time" and he wanted to get away from it.

He ducked down as he moved away from the helicopter, walking carefully, but without the need for his crutch. He had intended to go into the main house to tell Mrs. Forbes he was back, but stopped when he saw someone moving in the guest house. He changed direction and went in the door. "Who's there?"

"Well, well, well," James said as he came out of the office carrying a stack of papers. "The walking wounded have returned."

He knew that James had been discharged last night, but he'd thought James was spending time on the mainland before he returned. But he was back and looking as fit as ever. "Talk about the walking wounded," Ethan said and crossed to the other man in greeting.

They shook hands, then Ethan slapped James on the shoulder. "Good to have you back. You look great."

James flicked his gaze over Ethan and shook his head. "Besides the attractive little cast you have on your leg, you look like hell."

Ethan hadn't slept well over the past three nights since the emergency with James. He was anxious to have the party over and incredibly restless. On top of that, he kept waking in his bed and found himself reaching for Morgan. He hated that the memories of being with her wouldn't just go away. They'd been together in that room for only hours, not even a full night, yet somehow, it seemed wrong to be in there without her.

Unable to discuss his feelings with his friend, he told James a partial truth. "It's the damn reception for Joe. It's taking over my life."

"You're not around, so that doesn't work. But that'll be done in a day or so, then you can get back to whatever it is your life has become."

Ethan looked sharply at James, thinking he was being sarcastic, but found the man smiling at him. "And what has my life become?"

"Success and business and broken legs."

"Leg, singular, thank you," he muttered and crossed to the doors that led to the deck. There hadn't been any rain for days, but fog was a constant. It lifted enough during the day, but as soon as night came, it dropped like a suffocating cloak over the island. "The fog's driving me nuts."

"What else is going on that's driving you nuts?"

He opened the doors and stepped out into bone-chilling cold. What was driving him nuts? He had his answer when he looked down at the beach and found himself hoping that he'd see Morgan there. He'd kissed her that last time to make a point, to prove to himself that he could do it then let her go. She felt sorry for him? He was like Bartholomew? He gripped the damp railing. The beach was empty. And he remembered that kiss with an aching clarity.

"When are you going to stop talking about the fog and tell me about the doctor?" James pushed.

Ethan closed his eyes tightly. "What about the doctor? He put on a new cast, and it's going to be on short term."

"No, Morgan."

He almost flinched at the sound of her name, but he didn't turn. He kept his eyes closed so tightly lights exploded behind his lids. "What about her?"

James was behind him, probably in the doorway, but Ethan didn't look. "You tell me."

Finally Ethan spun around, and had to steady himself before he could speak. "Tell you what?"

James studied him. "I saw you with her. I'm not stupid. You tell me what's going on, or what's not going on."

Ethan took a breath and told him everything. When he finished, James straightened. "And?"

"Nothing. It's over and done."

"Just like that? You're going to let all of this go just so the damn board doesn't dislike you?"

"Hey, that's not—"

"Hell it isn't. Since when have you been afraid of the board? It's your damn company."

"You don't understand—"

James threw up his hands. "You know what—I'm leaving."

"Go ahead," Ethan said, thankful to have him leave with his questions in tow.

"No, I mean for good. I've had it. I've seen you with women like Natalie and how shallow it all was. But with the doctor..." He shook his head. "Dammit, haven't you noticed what Joe and Alegra are like when they're together? That's what you could have."

Ethan stared at James. He didn't know what he could or couldn't have.

"Why don't you take a chance, even if you lose control of the damn corporation, and do the right thing by everyone?"

Ethan hesitated. "Or?"

"If you don't, I'm quitting."

Christmas Eve

MORGAN WAS ABOVE in the back room of the medical offices packing textbooks. She was functioning and actually thought she might have found a building that could do temporarily for their clinic. It was too small and not what they needed in the long run, but it just might fill in the gap until she found a place where they could eventually settle. The house was a different matter. Any home on the island that was close enough to wherever the office ended up being would be fine—old or new—as long as the location fit.

She picked up a thick book that she remembered from her college days, and saw a glittery piece of paper flutter to the floor. She bent to retrieve it and looked down at an elegant gold-and-silver invitation with swirling script. *You are invited to joyously celebrate the first day of our new life together at the home of Ethan Grace.* Under it was a date and time, and a signature done by hand. *Alegra and Joe.* She had no idea why it was there. Maybe Sharon had a copy of it.

Morgan sank down on the only chair in the storage space and stared at the heavy paper. She'd heard about the party, that it had been a huge success and that Alegra, Joe and Alex were in their new home down the road from the old lighthouse.

"Joyously celebrate," she whispered. The words made her ache and she had to stop. She put the paper facedown on one of the books and closed her eyes. "Stop it," she told herself, trying to focus on anything but Ethan.

She turned back to the packing, determinedly reading the titles of the books out loud to fill the emptiness. Then another sound echoed through the offices. Someone was at the door, knocking hard. She pushed the books aside, got up and brushed at the jeans and green flannel shirt she was wearing, then tucking her loose hair behind her ears, she headed toward the front.

She could make out the silhouette of a large figure through the frosted glass and reached for the handle. "Who's there?"

She was stunned when she heard, "James Evans."

She fumbled with the lock, then pulled the door open and came face-to-face with the man. He looked incredible. "James. You look terrific. Come on in," she said, and stepped back to give him access to the waiting room.

He shook his head. "No, thanks. I just came to tell you in person how grateful I am for everything you did for me."

"You're very welcome. Dr. Perry said you were going to be just fine."

"Yes, I am, as long as I follow the rules." He shrugged. "Better to follow rules than go through that again."

"Absolutely."

"I need to get going, but I wanted to wish you a very Merry Christmas and give you this." He held out a large envelope.

She started to say she didn't want any payment, but that wasn't true; she needed all the money they could get for the future. "Thank you, and Merry Christmas to you, too."

He glanced down at the envelope as she took it and said something she didn't quite understand. "That was hard-won," he said, "and hopefully it will change a few lives."

Before she could ask him what he meant, he nodded, then turned and walked off. After closing and locking the door, she pulled opened the envelope. She took out three heavy sheets of paper, but none of them were checks. Reading them, she couldn't believe what she was holding. The first sheet was a deed for the buildings and land where the medical offices and house stood, fully notarized and in the name of her father and her. The second sheet was another deed for the empty land to the north. Her name and her father's were clearly written in black and white on the Name of Owner line.

Her hands were shaking so hard as she looked at the third sheet of paper she could barely read the words rendered in a bold script.

I am not Bartholomew and I take this oath. I will not pillage and plunder, and I will not destroy anymore.

It was signed with a scrawling signature that she'd seen before—Ethan Grace.

She dropped the papers to the floor when she turned to open the door and ran out into the foggy night.

Chapter Fourteen

Morgan stared out into the darkness in both directions, but a large black SUV was nowhere in sight. She exhaled, her chest so tight she was afraid she wouldn't be able to breathe again. James was gone. She had deeds with her and her father's names on them for the entire property. She could barely take it in. Turning to go back inside to try to figure out if she was hallucinating, she was stopped by a voice.

"One more thing," Ethan said. "I'm not Bartholomew in a very important way."

She had to be imagining things—the SUV parked by the side of the building, Ethan coming toward her, the papers lying on the floor in the waiting room. None of this could exist. Then he was closer, and she realized that even if this wasn't reality, she didn't care. She didn't want it to ever stop. "What's that?" she managed to say.

He walked with a limp, and she could see a smaller cast on his foot. "Bartholomew never cared about anyone but himself or what anyone thought about him."

She was holding her breath as he came closer and closer. The dark slacks and equally dark jacket he wore made him almost blend into the night. "What…what are you talking about?" she asked, the fog making her voice softly echo around them.

"The truth," he said, stopping a few feet from her.

"What is the truth?" she whispered, almost afraid to hear his answer.

"The truth is, you were right. I do destroy, and I've been destroying myself in the process."

She shook her head, barely able to assimilate what he was saying. "You, no," she said, and found she had to hug herself to keep any semblance of control. "The deeds and you here?"

"I want you to have the offices and the house, and the land. No matter what we would do with them, it wouldn't serve the island, or your family, as well as it would if you stayed here and built your clinic. It's the best use of the land by far."

It was a miracle, a real miracle, and she couldn't understand how it could have happened. "Why?" was all she could get out. "Why?"

He came closer, so close, but didn't touch her. "Because of you. Because of what you've brought into my life. Things I didn't even know were there until you were gone." He chuckled, a rough sound that had more irony in it than humor. "Who would have thought that James understood everything all long before I did?"

"James?" She was shaking now and she wanted nothing more than to hold Ethan. Real or not, she wanted to feel herself in his arms one more time.

But he kept that distance between them intact. "It's a long story, but let's just say he threatened to quit if I didn't get a clue about what I really wanted and what I was really feeling. And he was right. That's why I'm here, to tell you the truth, a truth I just admitted to myself."

She looked toward the open office door and moved away from Ethan, heading for it. She didn't want to listen to any of this. The only truth she knew right then was that she loved

Ethan and it hadn't diminished. It had only grown while they'd been apart. And she wanted it to stop.

ETHAN HAD KNOWN this wouldn't be easy, but he hadn't expected her to run into the offices and leave him standing alone in the parking lot. He went after her. He'd come this far and he wasn't going anywhere without telling her why he was there.

He stepped into the waiting room with the Christmas lights twinkling all around. Morgan was crouched on the floor, picking up papers he knew were the deeds and his note. She stood and looked shocked to see that he'd followed her. Her hair was loose around her shoulders, and with no makeup, she looked endearingly young. "This cast is a lot lighter and I can actually walk at an almost normal pace," he said to fill the awkward silence between them.

She glanced down at his foot, then did something that made no sense. She held the papers out to him, and said, "Here. Take them back."

He was stunned. He hadn't been exactly sure how she'd react to his actions, but this was the last thing he'd expected. "What are you talking about? They're yours. Legally yours. E.P.G. doesn't have any claim on them any longer."

"Why?" she asked.

"I told you I came to tell you the truth and I will."

She stared at him but didn't speak. She was crushing the papers in her hands, but he didn't mention that to her. Instead, he fought against the feeling that the next few minutes would change his life forever.

"When Joe and Alegra got married, Joe said something that hit me hard. He said he was terrified that he'd never find that other part of himself that would make him whole. Then he found Alegra."

The deeds would have to be redone, he thought, as she began twisting the papers now.

"What I came to say is, you're the other half of me I've been looking for all my life. The other half of me that makes me human. Very human."

She just stood there, staring at him, then silent tears started to roll down her cheeks. She didn't move to brush them away, and when she trembled, he couldn't maintain the distance between them any longer. With a single stride, he came within inches of her. He was so close that he saw a tear hang on her spiked lash before falling softly down her face. "I need you," he said. "Please don't send me away."

He was experiencing so many new feelings, and it had all begun with this woman. He was used to being in control, not to backing down, to never being afraid. But right then, he had no control, he would back down from anything to make her happy and he was afraid that he was too late.

"Oh, Ethan," she whispered, dropping the papers.

He framed her face with his hands and was shaking as much as she had been moments ago. "I'm not used to begging, but I need you in my world to help me figure out how to make things, to nourish things. More importantly, how to love one person with all my heart and soul. I need a miracle."

"I'm not a miracle worker," she choked out.

"Oh, yes, you are. You worked miracles on me in so many ways. But I need more healing. I need you." He looked into her eyes and finally said the basic truth that lived in him. "I love you."

Those three words changed everything. She was suddenly in his arms, holding tightly to him, and he heard her speak, but her voice was muffled against his chest. He eased her back and brushed at a single tear on her cheek. "What?" he asked.

She looked up at him, and said, "I have loved you for forever."

He pulled her against him and whispered roughly, "Thank you, thank you."

He looked over her at the Christmas tree and saw the angel on top. It was leaning to one side, its halo at a cockeyed angle over one eye, and he grinned. Miracles really did happen. He kissed Morgan and knew that all the time he'd been running in every direction in his life, the only direction he should have gone was back here to find her.

"Merry Christmas," he heard himself breathe, and he meant it for the first time in his life.

Morgan actually laughed. "Now that's a miracle."

"See? I told you you were a terrific doctor, that you dealt in miracles. I'm the living proof of that."

The Day After Christmas

IN THE DARKNESS of Morgan's bedroom where she'd spent her youth, she lay with Ethan in the old spindle bed. She was in his arms, exhausted; but so happy she couldn't even begin to put her feelings into words. They'd been together since Christmas Eve, had shared Christmas Day, even having a turkey and cranberry sauce that Ethan had loved. It had been takeout, but delicious. And their present to each other was that time together. The real miracle was that she hadn't had one emergency call in all that time. The offices were closed until the next day, and she didn't plan on leaving the house until then.

It was near midnight when she stirred and kissed Ethan as she curled into his side, loving the sound of his heartbeat under her palm. He had a heart, and it wasn't two sizes too small after all. The deeds were put away in the office, but the most important thing in her life was right here in bed with her. Loving Ethan and knowing that he loved her made her smile and feel blessed.

He shifted, and his fingers trailed up her arm, teasing the skin with a feathery touch that made her tremble. "I thought you were asleep," he said through the shadows.

"If you touch me like that, how do you expect me to sleep?" she said and turned to press a kiss to his chest.

"And that's bad?" he breathed, caressing her breast and laughing softly when she gasped at the contact. "No sleep," he whispered and took her again.

With the smaller cast, he rolled on top of her, and their joining was as natural and as wonderful as if they'd been together for years and years. He seemed to know her, what she wanted, what she needed, and when he was in her, she welcomed him, taking everything he had to give. They climaxed together.

"There's something I want to say, but have never quite found the right time," he began, raising himself on one elbow and looking down at her.

She brushed his cheek with her fingers and felt the roughness of a new beard. "Is it serious?" she asked with a touch of apprehension.

"Very serious."

Her hand stilled. She swallowed. "Okay, what is it?"

"This is terrific, but it can't last," he said, and she drew back, suddenly feeling cold.

She caught the sheet and pulled it over herself as she turned away from Ethan. Staring up at the ceiling, she waited until he spoke again. "I think Bartholomew was right about one thing."

She didn't care about Bartholomew or if he was right or wrong about anything. "Oh?" was all she said.

"The old guy knew that Shelter Island was his safe harbor. Although I grew up here and lived here off and on, it never felt like that to me. Not until now." He reached for her hand that crushed the sheet to her breasts. "Not until you. Now the island's more than that. It's home."

She looked at him. "Then what's wrong?"

He drew her hand to him, making her drop the sheet. "I just wanted to tell you that I love you and, if you'll have me, I want to marry you."

She heard the words, and they filtered into her soul. "That…that's a problem?" she asked.

He pressed her palm to his heart. "It is if you say no."

She felt his frantic heartbeat under her touch and actually laughed at him. It felt good, so good. "Oh, Ethan, I was going to ask you to marry me if you didn't ask me."

He laughed with her, pulling her into his arms. "Thank God! Yes, I'll marry you," he said.

"And I'll marry you," she answered. "When?"

The phone rang for the first time in three days, and the sound was jarring in the small bedroom. She was tempted to ignore it, but couldn't. "I have to," she said to Ethan.

"Do it." After a quick kiss, he stretched to grab the receiver and offer it to her.

"Dr. Kelly."

"Dr. Kelly here, too," her father said with a laugh.

"Oh, Dad," she said.

"Merry Christmas, honey. I was going to call on Christmas Day, but I know how busy you are on the holidays."

She turned and looked at Ethan, whose eyes were on her. "Yes, they've been pretty busy."

"Any problems?"

"Not one," she said with heartfelt truthfulness. "And I've got a few presents for you."

"We'll have a gift-giving evening when I get back, and when I get your gifts wrapped."

"I don't need my gifts wrapped," she said, and Ethan grinned at her.

"Of course you do," he said. "I just hate for you to be there all alone."

"I'm just fine," she said, and let Ethan take her free hand in his. "In fact, I'm perfect."

Her father hesitated and seemed to be more perceptive then she'd ever thought he was. "What's going on?"

She got closer to Ethan, lying by his side. "I have a couple of gifts for you when you get back."

"And?"

"And you'll have to wait until then. But I promise that you'll love them." She met Ethan's gaze.

"Honey, don't you work too hard."

"Sure, of course," she said and closed her eyes when Ethan cupped her naked breast in his hand. "I need to go. I've got something important to take care of."

"Okay, no problem. I'll see you next week."

"I can't wait," she said and hung up.

Ethan took the phone from her, put it back in the cradle then turned back to her. "Some presents?" he asked.

She smiled at him. "Sure. The deeds and you. Dad will be ecstatic about both, but mostly, I suspect, about you when he sees how much I love you."

She kissed him on the arm and saw the dark shape of the tattoo there. She traced it with her fingertip. "I would have never suspected that you'd be the tattoo type."

He circled her with his arm and held her tightly. "College, too much beer, a night by the docks. The next morning I had that and no idea how it got there."

"Do it?" she asked, reading the words permanently etched on his biceps.

"Now that I agree with," he said. "That's why I kept it all these years." He touched his lips to her forehead. "Do it."

She propped herself up on her elbow and gazed down at him. "When?"

"When what?"

"The small, private wedding that won't have someone like Roz running roughshod over everyone in sight?"

He didn't hesitate. "The sooner the better. Las Vegas, Mexico or the guest house."

"You mean it? We could get married in the guest house?"

"Sure. Why not? Family, James, a few friends and a minister or judge. We'd have all we need."

She had all she needed right there, right then. "Yes, let's do it, and I think that it's time for me to stay put."

"How so?"

"Here, on the island. This is where I belong. Dad can cut back his hours and I can take over some for him. He can take care of the plans for the new clinic and Sharon can redo the offices. And I can love you. Can you rearrange your work so we don't have to leave here too often?"

"Absolutely. James has wanted more responsibility from the start, and I think it's time to let him." He touched her face. "Meanwhile, I'll be at home with my doctor."

"Perfect," she said and never meant anything more in her life. Home. With Ethan. It was perfect.

* * * * *

**Every Life Has More
Than One Chapter**

Award-winning author Stevi Mittman delivers another
hysterical mystery, featuring Teddi Bayer, an irrepress-
ible heroine, and her to-die-for hero, Detective Drew
Scoones. After all, life on Long Island can be murder!

*Turn the page for a sneak peek at the warm and funny
fourth book,
WHOSE NUMBER IS UP, ANYWAY?,
in the Teddi Bayer series,
by STEVI MITTMAN.
On sale August 7*

"Before redecorating a room, I always advise my clients to empty it of everything but one chair. Then I suggest they move that chair from place to place, sitting in it, until the placement feels right. Trust your instincts when deciding on furniture placement. Your room should "feel right."

—TipsFromTeddi.com

Gut feelings. You know, that gnawing in the pit of your stomach that warns you that you are about to do the absolute stupidest thing you could do? Something that will ruin life as you know it?

I've got one now, standing at the butcher counter in King Kullen, the grocery store in the same strip mall as L.I. Lanes, the bowling alley cum billiard parlor I'm in the process of re-decorating for its "Grand Opening."

I realize being in the wrong supermarket probably doesn't sound exactly dire to you, but you aren't the one buying your father a brisket at a store your mother will somehow know isn't Waldbaum's.

And then, June Bayer isn't your mother.

The woman behind the counter has agreed to go into the freezer to find a brisket for me, since there aren't any in the case. There are packages of pork tenderloin, piles of spare ribs and rolls of sausage, but no briskets.

Warning Number Two, right? I should be so out of here.

But no, I'm still in the same spot when she comes back out, brisketless, her face ashen. She opens her mouth as if she is going to scream, but only a gurgle comes out.

And then she pinballs out from behind the counter, knocking bottles of Peter Luger Steak Sauce to the floor on her way, now hitting the tower of cans at the end of the prepared foods aisle and sending them sprawling, now making her way down the aisle, careening from side to side as she goes.

Finally, from a distance, I hear her shout, "He's deeeeeaaaad! Joey's deeeeeaaaad."

My first thought is *You should always trust your gut.*

My second thought is that now, somehow, my mother will know I was in King Kullen. For weeks I will have to hear "What did you expect?" as though whenever you go to King Kullen someone turns up dead. And if the detective investigating the case turns out to be Detective Drew Scoones... well, I'll never hear the end of that from her, either.

She still suspects I murdered the guy who was found dead on my doorstep last Halloween just to get Drew back into my life.

Several people head for the butcher's freezer and I position myself to block them. If there's one thing I've learned from finding people dead—and the guy on my doorstep wasn't the first one—it's that the police get very testy when you mess with their murder scenes.

"You can't go in there until the police get here," I say, stationing myself at the end of the butcher's counter and in front of the Employees Only door, acting as if I'm some sort of authority. "You'll contaminate the evidence if it turns out to be murder."

Shouts and chaos. You'd think I'd know better than to throw the word *murder* around. Cell phones are flipping open and tongues are wagging.

I amend my statement quickly. "Which, of course, it probably isn't. Murder, I mean. People die all the time, and it's not always in hospitals or their own beds, or…" I babble when I'm nervous, and the idea of someone dead on the other side of the freezer door makes me very nervous.

So does the idea of seeing Drew Scoones again. Drew and I have this on-again, off-again sort of thing…that I kind of turned off.

Who knew he'd take it so personally when he tried to get serious and I responded by saying we could talk about *us* tomorrow—and then caught a plane to my parents' condo in Boca the next day? In July. In the middle of a job.

For some crazy reason, he took that to mean that I was avoiding him and the subject of *us*.

That was three months ago. I haven't seen him since.

The manager, who identifies himself and points to his nameplate in case I don't believe him, says he has to go into *his cooler*. "Maybe Joey's not dead," he says. "Maybe he can be saved, and you're letting him die in there. Did you ever think of that?"

In fact, I hadn't. But I had thought that the murderer might try to go back in to make sure his tracks were covered, so I say that I will go in and check.

Which means that the manager and I couple up and go in together while everyone pushes against the doorway to peer in, erasing any chance of finding clean prints on that Employee Only door.

I expect to find carcasses of dead animals hanging from

hooks, and maybe Joey hanging from one, too. I think it's going to be very creepy and I steel myself, only to find a rather benign series of shelves with large slabs of meat laid out carefully on them, along with boxes and boxes marked simply Chicken.

Nothing scary here, unless you count the body of a middle-aged man with graying hair sprawled faceup on the floor. His eyes are wide open and unblinking. His shirt is stiff. His pants are stiff. His body is stiff. And his expression, you should forgive the pun—is frozen. Bill-the-manager crosses himself and stands mute while I pronounce the guy dead in a sort of *happy now?* tone.

"We should not be in here," I say, and he nods his head emphatically and helps me push people out of the doorway just in time to hear the police sirens and see the cop cars pull up outside the big store windows.

Bobbie Lyons, my partner in Teddi Bayer Interior Designs (and also my neighbor, my best friend and my private fashion police), and Mark, our carpenter (and my dogsitter, confidant, and ego booster), rush in from next door. They beat the cops by a half step and shout out my name. People point in my direction.

After all the publicity that followed the unfortunate incident during which I shot my ex-husband, Rio Gallo, and then the subsequent murder of my first client—which I solved, I might add—it seems like the whole world, or at least all of Long Island, knows who I am.

Mark asks if I'm all right. (Did I remember to mention that the man is drop-dead-gorgeous-but-a-decade-too-young-for-me-yet-too-old-for-my-daughter-thank-god?) I don't get a chance to answer him because the police are quickly closing in on the store manager and me.

"The woman—" I begin telling the police. Then I have to

pause for the manager to fill in her name, which he does: *Fran*.

I continue. "Right. Fran. Fran went into the freezer to get a brisket. A moment later she came out and screamed that Joey was dead. So I'd say she was the one who discovered the body."

"And you are…?" the cop asks me. It comes out a bit like who do I *think* I am, rather than who am I really?

"An innocent bystander," Bobbie, hair perfect, makeup just right, says, carefully placing her body between the cop and me.

"And she was just leaving," Mark adds. They each take one of my arms.

Fran comes into the inner circle surrounding the cops. In case it isn't obvious from the hairnet and bloodstained white apron with Fran embroidered on it, I explain that she was the butcher who was going for the brisket. Mark and Bobbie take that as a signal that I've done my job and they can now get me out of there. They twist around, with me in the middle, as if we're a Rockettes line, until we are facing away from the butcher counter. They've managed to propel me a few steps toward the exit when disaster—in the form of a Mazda RX7 pulling up at the loading curb—strikes.

Mark's grip on my arm tightens like a vise. "Too late," he says.

Bobbie's expletive is unprintable. "Maybe there's a back door," she suggests, but Mark is right. It's too late.

I've laid my eyes on Detective Scoones. And while my gut is trying to warn me that my heart shouldn't go there, regions farther south are melting at just the sight of him.

"Walk," Bobbie orders me.

And I try to. Really.

Walk, I tell my feet. *Just put one foot in front of the other.*

I can do this because I know, in my heart of hearts, that if

Drew Scoones was still interested in me, he'd have gotten in touch with me after I returned from Boca. And he didn't.

Since he's a detective, Drew doesn't have to wear one of those dark blue Nassau County Police uniforms. Instead, he's got on jeans, a tight-fitting T-shirt and a tweedy sports jacket. If you think that sounds good, you should see him. Chiseled features, cleft chin, brown hair that's naturally a little sandy in the front, a smile that…well, that doesn't matter. He isn't smiling now.

He walks up to me, tucks his sunglasses into his breast pocket and looks me over from head to toe.

"Well, if it isn't Miss Cut and Run," he says. "Aren't you supposed to be somewhere in Florida or something?" He looks at Mark accusingly, as if he was covering for me when he told Drew I was gone.

"Detective Scoones?" one of the uniforms says. "The stiff's in the cooler and the woman who found him is over there." He jerks his head in Fran's direction.

Drew continues to stare at me.

You know how when you were young, your mother always told you to wear clean underwear in case you were in an accident? And how, a little farther on, she told you not to go out in hair rollers because you never knew who you might see—or who might see you? And how now your best friend says she wouldn't be caught dead without makeup and suggests you shouldn't either?

Okay, today, *finally,* in my overalls and Converse sneakers, I get it.

I brush my hair out of my eyes. "Well, I'm back," I say. As if he hasn't known my exact whereabouts. The man is a detective, for heaven's sake. "Been back awhile."

Bobbie has watched the exchange and apparently decided she's given Drew all the time he deserves. "And we've got work to do, so…" she says, grabbing my arm and giving Drew a little two-fingered wave goodbye.

As I back up a foot or two, the store manager sees his chance and places himself in front of Drew, trying to get his attention. Maybe what makes Drew such a good detective is his ability to focus.

Only what he's focusing on is me.

"Phone broken? Carrier pigeon died?" he asks me, taking in Fran, the manager, the meat counter and that Employees Only door, all without taking his eyes off me.

Mark tries to break the spell. "We've got work to do there, you've got work to do here, Scoones," Mark says to him, gesturing toward next door. "So it's back to the alley for us."

Drew's lip twitches. "You working the alley now?" he says.

"If you'd like to follow me," Bill-the-manager, clearly exasperated, says to Drew—who doesn't respond. It's as if waiting for my answer is all he has to do.

So, fine. "You knew I was back," I say.

The man has known my whereabouts every hour of the day for as long as I've known him. And my mother's not the only one who won't buy that he "just happened" to answer this particular call. In fact, I'm willing to bet my children's lunch money that he's taken every call within ten miles of my home since the day I got back.

And now he's gotten lucky.

"*You* could have called *me*," I say.

"You're the one who said *tomorrow* for our talk and then flew the coop, chickie," he says. "I figured the ball was in your court."

"Detective?" the uniform says. "There's something you ought to see in here."

Drew gives me a look that amounts to *in or out?*

He could be talking about the investigation, or about our relationship.

Bobbie tries to steer me away. Mark's fists are balled. Drew waits me out, knowing I won't be able to resist what might be a murder investigation.

Finally he turns and heads for the cooler.

And, like a puppy dog, I follow.

Bobbie grabs the back of my shirt and pulls me to a halt.

"I'm just going to show him something," I say, yanking away.

"Yeah," Bobbie says, pointedly looking at the buttons on my blouse. The two at breast level have popped. "That's what I'm afraid of."

REQUEST YOUR FREE BOOKS!
2 FREE NOVELS PLUS 2
FREE GIFTS!

American **ROMANCE®**

Heart, Home & Happiness!

YES! Please send me 2 FREE Harlequin American Romance® novels and my 2 FREE gifts. After receiving them, if I don't wish to receive any more books, I can return the shipping statement marked "cancel." If I don't cancel, I will receive 4 brand-new novels every month and be billed just $4.24 per book in the U.S., or $4.99 per book in Canada, plus 25¢ shipping and handling per book and applicable taxes, if any*. That's a savings of close to 15% off the cover price! I understand that accepting the 2 free books and gifts places me under no obligation to buy anything. I can always return a shipment and cancel at any time. Even if I never buy another book from Harlequin, the two free books and gifts are mine to keep forever.

154 HDN EEZK 354 HDN EEZV

Name _____ (PLEASE PRINT)

Address _____ Apt. #

City _____ State/Prov. _____ Zip/Postal Code

Signature (if under 18, a parent or guardian must sign)

Mail to the **Harlequin Reader Service®**:
IN U.S.A.: P.O. Box 1867, Buffalo, NY 14240-1867
IN CANADA: P.O. Box 609, Fort Erie, Ontario L2A 5X3

Not valid to current Harlequin American Romance subscribers.

Want to try two free books from another line?
Call 1-800-873-8635 or visit www.morefreebooks.com.

* Terms and prices subject to change without notice. NY residents add applicable sales tax. Canadian residents will be charged applicable provincial taxes and GST. This offer is limited to one order per household. All orders subject to approval. Credit or debit balances in a customer's account(s) may be offset by any other outstanding balance owed by or to the customer. Please allow 4 to 6 weeks for delivery.

Your Privacy: Harlequin is committed to protecting your privacy. Our Privacy Policy is available online at www.eHarlequin.com or upon request from the Reader Service. From time to time we make our lists of customers available to reputable firms who may have a product or service of interest to you. If you would prefer we not share your name and address, please check here. ☐

HAR07

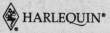

HARLEQUIN®

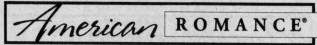

American ROMANCE®

TEXAS LEGACIES:
THE CARRIGANS

Get to the Heart of a Texas Family

WITH

THE RANCHER NEXT DOOR
by
Cathy Gillen Thacker

She'll Run The Ranch—And Her Life—Her Way!

On her alpaca ranch in Texas, Rebecca encounters
constant interference from Trevor McCabe, the
bossy rancher next door. Rebecca becomes very
friendly with Vince Owen, her other neighbor and
Trevor's archrival from college. Trevor's problem
is convincing Rebecca that he is on her side, and
aware of Vince's ulterior motives. But Trevor has
fallen for her in the process....

On sale July 2007

COMING NEXT MONTH

#1173 MOMMY FOR A MINUTE by Judy Christenberry
Dallas Duets
When Jack Mason came to renovate her apartment with his toddler in tow, Lauren McNabb fell for Ally—and the handsome Jack. But Jack didn't want "The Shark," as she was known in legal circles, around his child. Lauren was beautiful and, after years of being alone, kissing her felt like heaven. But could the workaholic be a mother…and a wife?

#1174 MITCH TAKES A WIFE by Ann Roth
To Wed, or Not To Wed
Fran Bishop, owner of the Oceanside B and B, has always wanted a husband and kids, but meeting men in the sleepy town of Cranberry, Oregon, isn't the easiest thing in the world. When longtime guest Mitch Matthews comes for his annual visit, Fran has no idea that their friendship is about to change—into something more permanent!

#1175 RYAN'S RENOVATION by Marin Thomas
The McKade Brothers
Brooding Ryan McKade had planned to complete his stint with a demolition company, thereby meeting his grandfather's requirement and assuring his inheritance, then be on his way. He sure as heck hadn't planned to fall for the company's secretary. Anna Nowakowski's cheery personality and trusting nature make him want to stay around longer. Except, then he'd have to reveal a few secrets—and would she still want him after he did?

#1176 GEORGIA ON HIS MIND by Ann DeFee
Win Whittaker, a top-level defense attorney from D.C., comes to Magnolia Bluffs, Georgia, on a bet. With only a hundred bucks in his pocket, he has to survive for a month. Which means he needs a job. It so happens that Kenni MacAllister's salon, Permanently Yours, has an opening for a shampoo girl. And that's how it all begins….

www.eHarlequin.com

HARCNM0707